THE TALE OF THE
OLD
SCHOOL TIES

GEORGE MURRAY

GEORGE MURRAY
PUBLICATIONS

THE TALE OF THE OLD SCHOOL TIES
(Mindless Motive)

Is the intellectual property of the author
GEORGE MURRAY
All rights reserved 2012 © George Murray

Cover design, typesetting and logo design by
PAULA HÖRLING-MOSES
www.macmoses.net

Cover photos by
www.shutterstock.com

Printed in the United Kingdom by
LIGHTNING SOURCE UK LTD
Milton Keynes

Published by
GEORGE MURRAY PUBLICATIONS
Edinburgh
April 2014

ISBN 978-0-9927385-6-3

The novel is entirely a work of fiction.
The names, characters and incidents portrayed in it are
the work of the author's imagination. Any resemblance to actual
persons, living or dead, events or localities is entirely coincidental.

THE TALE OF THE OLD SCHOOL TIES

GEORGE MURRAY

"Æquam memento rebus in arduis servare mentem"

HORACE (QUINTUS HORATIUS FLACCUS)
LATIN POET
40 BC

*"In times of stress,
in times of need,
do not panic,
keep the heid"*

JOCK (THOMSON) OF GLASGOW
PUBLIC TOILET POET
MUCH LATER

PROLOGUE

This story concerns the abduction and murder of three young school pupils from two separate independent schools in the south of England.

On the last day of the school year, for the past three years, a senior first form child has been taken from school and never seen alive again.

When black plastic bags containing body parts from child corpses begin to be found in the west highlands of Scotland, there is no immediate connection made.

The area is the home territory of Constable Andrew Fleming, a slightly disrespectful police officer, who nevertheless unravels the strange affair and traces a suspect.

With the benefit of natural intelligence and academic achievements, the killer has created a new life for himself, going to great lengths to conceal his true identity. His true identity, his history and his warped mind are the secret to unlocking the mystery of the murders. The killer has an inherited incapacity to deal with unforeseen adversity.

As Fleming breaks through the shell of concealment the killer is triggered to react badly and become a danger to more than schoolchildren. In Fleming's own words, 'This man is not stupid, but he is mad.'

ONE

The warm spring sunshine lit up the grand architecture of the old building and the neatly mowed lawns and trimmed hedges that surrounded it. Beyond the building and screened from it by great oak trees were the playing fields for cricket and rugby football. These playing fields were equally well maintained. The cost of outdoor maintenance was substantial but dwarfed by the overall running costs of Letherford School for boys in the county of Kent.

The beautiful building and the seventy acres surrounding it had once been the Letherford Tyndall Estate, but Lord Letherford, a retired sea captain, had bequeathed the property and twenty-five thousand pounds in 1805. He had instructed his trustees to create a seat of learning for 'young men capable of raising and maintaining the standard of British trade and endeavour'.

The bequest had been welcomed and properly executed. The initial years were everything that Lord Letherford would have envisaged through the remainder of the 19th century. The wars and depression of the 20th century had taken a serious toll on the staff and pupil numbers but matters had improved following the end of the Second World War. By the 1960's the status of the school had risen again to being a constant, steady provider of excellent alumni progressing to university colleges. Oxford and Cambridge were closer to Letherford School than any map might suggest.

The staff at the school had all been selected on the basis of their own personal merit in their specialist subjects and their known and proven ability to develop the same high standards and fortifying confidence in their pupils. Admission to Letherford was not based on finance alone. All entrants had demonstrated their own merit in admission examinations. The reputation of the establishment was everything; without that reputation the attraction of Letherford to the wealthy parents of capable children would quickly recede.

These very thoughts were the present nightmare of John Wetherby, the current headmaster of Letherford School, as he sat at his large oak desk in front of a tall bay window. He ought to be on summer vacation, as most of staff and pupils were. A few boys were still in school as their parents or guardians were not in a position to collect them, or who, for one reason or another preferred the boys to defer their journey home. The school roll was all on holiday with the exception of these few and the staff presence was similarly depleted. The boys at school were under the care temporarily of volunteering former staff members.

THE TALE OF THE OLD SCHOOL TIES

John Wetherby was a very troubled man who could see the precious reputation of this great school collapsing under his watch and his own personal prestige collapsing with it. His concern centred on a 12 year old boy from the first senior form, a boy called William Johnston Faraday. William should be among the small number of boys still in the school dormitories for these early days of the holidays. Like his parents, the boy was Australian although his father, Gerald Faraday, had once been a pupil at Letherford.

Young William Faraday had been missing for a few days. He had been seen last on Saturday 26th June, the day that school had broken up for summer recess.

This had made the boy's disappearance less obvious at the time and less alarming as possibilities existed for him to accompany some homeward bound friend briefly. That would be a breach of school rules but much less of a concern than his unexplained absence had since become. Each passing day made his disappearance more ominous and a safe explanation less likely. William had never suggested to his form master that he wished to attend some outside event or accompany anyone as they left to go home.

John Wetherby had realised that by the time he had been made aware of the boy Faraday's absence it was already time to report the matter to the police and the boy's parents in Australia.

Two years earlier, a pupil of the same age had gone

missing from the same school at the end of term and had never been found. The loss of young Richard Barton had brought levels of anxiety not previously considered possible at Letherford and school figures had dipped. A second missing pupil would have catastrophic repercussions for the school. The previous year had seen the disappearance of 12 year old girl pupil from a girl's school in Surrey. As far as Wetherby knew, the little girl, like Barton, had never been found.

In the circumstances his presence at the school was a matter of absolute necessity. He found himself fielding questions from anxious parents, politicians, pushy reporters and television journalists. He felt a mounting pressure as the raw mental savagery of a repeated nightmare occupied his consciousness. Every moment he found himself either sitting or standing without actually doing something, he felt a tremendous guilt and vulnerability.

The headmaster raised a switch on his telephone as he rose from his desk to leave. Any caller would now be informed that he away from his desk but would be paged to take the call. He left the main building and headed for the first form dormitory.

In the dorm he found four young lads idly playing around a pool table. The boys stopped when he entered.

"Sorry to interrupt your game boys but I am most concerned about young Faraday. There is still no word of him. Did any of you see him on the last day of school?"

THE TALE OF THE OLD SCHOOL TIES

The boys looked from one to another.

"I think we all saw him in the morning, sir." the tallest boy reported. "We told Mr Thomas, our form master. William was staying for the first week of the holiday as you know but he wanted to buy a maths set, a protractor, compasses and so on."

"Yes, I see. Did he say where he intended to do this?" John Wetherby asked.

"He said he would go into town for one." another boy answered. "But I don't know if he meant a town here or if he was going into London."

"He did have his school uniform on?" the headmaster asked.

"Yes sir." three boys said as one.

At that moment the headmaster's pager bleeped twice. He looked down at the number being displayed and went to the dormitory telephone where he dialled the access code to the incoming police call.

"Oh dear," he whispered as the latest development was described to him. "Can I call you back from my own office? I am at a dormitory just now."

"Is it William, sir?" the tall boy asked, having seen the headmaster's look of disappointment.

"No. William is still missing." Wetherby said, drawing himself erect and resuming his normal dignified appearance before striding out of the dormitory.

Apparently a parcel of blood-stained clothing had been found in a litter bin at a motorway service station. The clothing consisted of Letherford School uniform, each item of which bore a name tag with the name 'William J. Faraday'. For reasons of lost property and laundry, it was a school requirement that each item of school clothing should bear the identity of the owner.

As he returned to his office to be told the full details in privacy, John Wetherby felt physically sick. It seemed that his worst fears for the future prospects of Letherford School and for himself were about to be realised.

The police interest in the disappearance of William J. Faraday was intense. The fact that this boy could disappear on precisely the same day, in terms of the school year, as the boy Barton in 1980 and the girl, Helen Holloway, in 1981, pointed to a significant coincidence. Only the discovery of William's blood-stained uniform made his disappearance different but the inference of violence was immediate. The immense improbability of the coincidences made the police consider at this early stage that a motive of some type was being expressed. In order to comprehend this motive it was necessary to find the culprit. His or her motive was as individually sinister as the perpetrator.

The recovered clothing did not contain any maths set or anything else. The boy would have had money in his possession but there was none in the clothing.

Using the school location as a central point the police searched and enquired outwards in an ever increasing radius. William's school portrait photograph for that year was used as part of the descriptive narrative circulated to stationers, bus and train services, media and press. More specific enquiry was made at the more likely premises to have been reached by the boy prior to abduction. The headmaster provided home addresses for pupils who had left for home on holiday in order that fellow pupils could be as completely interviewed as possible as to their last sightings of William. Had he ordered a taxi? Had he shared a taxi? Had he accepted a lift? Answers were actively sought for these questions.

At the service area there was CCTV in use but the system did not cover the darkened places around the main building and fuel pumps. None gave an extended view towards the car park and the unattended litter bin where the clothing had been found. The available footage was taken in any event so that it could be scanned for all persons using the facility to purchase fuel or food. The litter bin and the clothing were seized by the police for forensic examination.

The school grounds and buildings were intimately searched by police teams with search dogs and plans were drawn up to cover vast areas of open farmland and empty commercial properties. Divers would coordinate their efforts in rivers, water courses and ponds to match the extent of dry land searching. Press and television and radio cover would ensure that the public were well aware of the missing schoolboy, William Johnston Faraday.

The staff at Eastward Grammar could not really understand Anthony Halbooth, now a third year pupil at the prestigious independent school in the suburbs of Glasgow, five hundred miles north from Letherford School and one hundred and twenty miles south from Halbooth's home near Corran Bay.

Anthony was the only child of two professors; his father was a lecturing biochemist with an international pharmaceutical company and his mother a pioneering archaeologist and consultant lecturer. With such a pedigree Anthony might be expected to breeze through the subjects of the curriculum with ease, his parents certainly expected him to do so. As a boy among other boys Anthony was still withdrawn and quiet, reluctant to participate in group exercises or discussions, he was serious to a fault and unable, or unwilling, to make friends.

He was attentive in class but it was when he was alone with a book that Anthony was at his best, detached from his surroundings and focussed entirely on the subject of the pages. His powers of concentration, where books and new class work were concerned far exceeded that of others. In the core subjects of maths, sciences and modern languages he excelled but it was in Latin and Greek that he was particularly outstanding.

Other pupils and staff saw him as a bit of an oddity, an extreme intellect. His teachers in these classical languages found him to be advanced but conversation with him tended to be one-sided. Only on the works of

Horace, Plato, Aristotle, Socrates or Virgil did Anthony show any enthusiasm to converse. He spoke of these long dead individuals as if they were present day acquaintances.

The parent – teacher evenings were never attended by both parents of Anthony Halbooth. Either Milton Halbooth or his wife Penelope would attend but occasionally neither did. When one of his parents did attend, the parental enquiries would be on his academic performance only. Neither parent had ever asked how Anthony, a boarding pupil, was faring among his peers. Was he well? Was he happy? Was he making friends? From the absence of such questions the staff had some insight into the behaviour of the boy.

For Anthony Halbooth, like Winston Churchill and countless others, the duration of his school education seemed like an emotional eviction from home, a convenient excuse to transfer responsibility and attention. Such feelings and sentiments could scarcely be attributed to everyone but staff could identify the boys for whom they did apply.

When the school broke for summer holidays on the last Saturday in June 1982, there was an influx of private cars to collect pupils and their luggage. Anthony Halbooth had ordered a taxi to take him to the railway station.

From an office window overlooking this exodus, the headmaster, Christopher Hamilton, watched Anthony Halbooth's departure.

Andrew Fleming was off-duty during the day and was quite happy to be leaning on his garden spade, talking to his neighbour about the merits of their respective cars. The neighbour was Duncan Hardisty, a professional photographer, who ran a Subaru estate car.

"I need a rugged motor that I can rely on." Duncan explained. "I have to be able to reach some pretty remote locations and in all sorts of weather. It's not all photographic equipment, you know Andy. I carry a sleeping bag, a gas cooker, pots, extra clothing and survival gear during the winter months."

"Is it worth the hassle?" Andy asked as if the obvious answer should be 'no'.

"Sometimes." Duncan replied with a smile.

"Only sometimes?" Andy said with a smile that suggested the answer was ridiculous.

"Yeah. Until I get there, I don't know whether my journey has been worth a photograph or not."

"Where is 'there'?" Fleming asked.

Duncan shrugged his shoulders.

"We all have our favourite places, Andy. Mine is Mull. It gives me a mountain, a castle, Tobermory waterfront and harbour, a couple of sea lochs and, of course, Iona. Then again, I like to go north to Torridon, Kyleakin or the Summer Isles. I might spend the day on Skye or get myself into Glencoe before dawn."

"You must be running up the miles on your Subaru, Duncan."

THE TALE OF THE OLD SCHOOL TIES

"It has about two hundred thousand miles on it at the moment, Andy." Duncan said with some pride.

"And you sometimes get a photo?" Andy commented with a hint of sarcasm.

"But when I do," Duncan said, raising a forefinger, "I get the one that everyone else wishes they had taken. I have the setting right, the sky is right, the air is clear, giving me the visibility I want and the next time I see my photograph, it is on a calendar or a biscuit tin or any number of postcards."

"Do you have to wait for the shot you are after?" Fleming asked, recalling a previous conversation with a newsreel cameraman.

"Yes, of course, but I prefer to be early and waiting than to being late for the perfect moment."

"There is such a moment?" Fleming asked, aware of his many discarded snapshots.

"Absolutely. If I go early or late on a shot I feel as if I have drawn second prize, Andy." Duncan said seriously.

"Does that happen to you much?"

"I am getting more intuitive with age," Duncan replied. "But sometimes fate plays a hand."

"The rain comes on." Fleming suggested.

"Perhaps, or a hare starts up out of the grass just as I am ready to button the shot, or the first car for three hours appears in an otherwise empty glen."

"That must be annoying." Fleming agreed.

"It is. It really is, but it happened to me the summer

before last up at Loch Levenside. I was all set up behind a rhododendron bush for a dawn shot of the bridge when this old banger came into the big dirt lay-by and parked right in the centre of my shot."

"So you aborted the shot?" Fleming suggested.

"Well no, as a matter of fact I took the shot and it was reasonable. The car was one of these old shooting brake things in dark green with the wood framing on the outside, remember them?"

"Yes, I do. They were good motors in their day, Duncan."

"Well that one was well-kept, so it didn't look too bad actually. I just wished it hadn't arrived when it did, or the driver had cleared off."

Fleming laughed and pointed to his own car.

"You don't have to go near Loch Leven to get a shot of a banger, Duncan. You can snap that old thing of mine any time you want."

Anthony Halbooth left the train station and pulled his wheeled suitcase behind him as he headed for the Corran Bay public library. The pleasant old lady behind the desk was not surprised to see him. School breaks were the only time she did see Anthony but he was a regular visitor during these breaks when he seemed to pass his time by borrowing, reading and returning books.

"What are you after this time?" Mrs Campbell asked in her quiet way as she noticed Anthony scouring the Roman/Greek section of the classical history shelves.

THE TALE OF THE OLD SCHOOL TIES

"The epodes of Horace from 23 BC or anything on Maecenas," the boy said quietly.

"Not on these shelves, Anthony, but wait 'til I check the system." she said as she turned back to her desk. A few taps on her keyboard and she looked up at Anthony with a smile. "It's there," she said in obvious delight. "I can have it here for you by Monday. Now Maecenas, let me see," she continued to tap the keyboard. "Only in a book on Augustus, do you want that one. It will take a week."

"Yes please."

Morton Grant was a strange individual, one of these unusual types that are said to exist in every community. He was employed by the local council in the capacity of painter and decorator and during working hours seemed pleasant and conscientious. Fleming had never seen Morton Grant really drunk but he knew that after a few pints of beer Morton could, and normally did, convert to an alter ego of his own choosing.

Andrew Fleming was not alone in his awareness of Morton's peculiarities. Mrs Campbell felt awkward whenever Morton made one of his occasional visits to the library but she hid her concerns behind her customary smile.

As Anthony Halbooth left the library, Morton Grant held the door open for him and stared into the boy's face. The student was young and slender while Morton was a heavy set man in his forties. In these circumstances it was a habit of Morton's to stare into the face of the smaller, younger person as if to intimidate that person. Anthony simply ignored him.

Morton went ahead and handed his book over to Mrs Campbell, returning her smile.

"So you have finished with the battle of the Little Bighorn, did you like it, Morton?"

"Aye, but I knew all about it anyway, my cousin was there. He was the only one to get away."

"Really?" Mrs Campbell replied with a genuine smile, prompted by her own thoughts, involving words like 'fruit' and 'cake', "So, what kind of book would you like now, Morton?"

"The Mafia." Morton replied with a worrying glint in his eye.

"Over there, Morton, in the blue section, on the right, about three shelves down from the top."

As Morton headed for the blue section Mrs Campbell shook her head. Over the next three weeks Morton's 'cousin' would be involved in contract killings and all manner of gangster activity and, after a few pints, Morton might well accompany him.

It was fully two miles from the library to the Halbooth residence, a sandstone lodge behind a high beech hedge. There were outhouses too, a reminder of bygone days when laundry, horses and hired help required separate accommodation.

Anthony trudged to the back door and tried to open it. It was locked, as he expected, so he left his case and went to the ivy covered outhouse that had once served as the washroom. From a concealed hook he obtained the box lock key that would allow him into his home. From behind the locked door of the laundry room there was a constant buzzing sound and Anthony noticed bluebottles flying in and out beneath the solid door.

Inside the house itself things were much as they had been when he had left, with little indication that anyone had been living there in the interim. The place would be dirty if not for the efforts of Mrs Gretchen MacIntyre, the lady from Corran Bay who came out three mornings of each week to perform two hours of housework.

After checking for any mail left for him and finding none, Anthony took his suitcase upstairs to his room and threw himself down on his bed. His room was just as he had left it, pretty much, in fact, as it had always been. It was no surprise or disappointment to him that he had come home to an empty house. His parents, in their separate and independent lives, were little more than occasional visitors themselves. Mrs MacIntyre came in Mondays, Wednesdays and Fridays. Today was Saturday and, judging by the small number of cobwebs around the keyhole in the ivy, Mrs MacIntyre had been the last person in the house. He stared up at the ceiling, at the notice that he had pinned up there when he started at Eastward Grammar. In blue and red felt marker pens it read, 'NO PAIN, NO GAIN'.

Anthony spent his first afternoon at home in peaceful solitude, revising the first and second battles of Philippi in 43 BC where victory had gone the way of Marc Anthony and Octavian over the forces of Brutus and Cassius. This result had been regarded by many as revenge for the death of Julius Caesar.

The weather was hot and Anthony opened his bedroom window a little. From time to time as he read he was distracted by the buzzing sound from the direction of the laundry door. Such distractions were irritating and he closed the window to shut out the noise. That would normally have sufficed but he knew about the bluebottles and his curiosity had been aroused. Until he had resolved the question of the bluebottles he could not hope to concentrate in his usual way.

He went outside to the cobbled courtyard and crossed to the laundry room where he knew that the door was always locked and the only person with a key for the place was his father. The window glass was white-washed from the inside and he could see nothing through the window. Was there a back window? He had no idea. He climbed onto the wall passing behind the building, hard against the wall of the building itself, making the presence of a window unlikely but he climbed up onto the wall anyway.

He walked along the wall behind the laundry and discovered a small rusty skylight in the slated roof where direct sunlight was shining into the laundry. He climbed onto the roof and tried to look through the green film on the glass. Using his handkerchief and some saliva, he rubbed a hole in the green obstruction until he could see the heavy wooden table beneath the window. There was an open box on the table and the contents of the box were covered in a moving mass of maggots. Anthony considered opening the skylight window but the rust had formed a union between the surfaces of the frame making it well-nigh impossible to open the window without causing damage. His father had presumably run over some poor animal on the road and brought it home in a box. Left in the laundry room, it had been forgotten about and remained unburied. Quite typical of his father's behaviour. Anthony climbed down and returned to the house and his studies. He tossed the dirty handkerchief into the laundry basket on his way to his room.

That Saturday evening Constable Andrew Fleming was on duty in Corran Bay where the various licensed venues were obliged to close at midnight. Only the occasional late licence, granted by the licensing authority for one particular evening, could permit intrusion into the Sabbath morning. None were in force that Saturday evening and Fleming's mind was more occupied with his later mission. In his pocket he had a handwritten note from Chief Inspector Stewart MacKellar which read simply, 'Dick inward 3 a.m.'.

This instruction meant that Fleming would attend a local airstrip at three in the morning to pick up a military intelligence officer from Northern Ireland who would be delivered to the rendezvous by helicopter. Fleming had been attending to this particular duty for some time and come to know 'Dick' as well as he was ever likely to.

In the meantime he noticed another familiar face stepping towards him. Morton Grant was approaching with an occasional glance towards Fleming. The police officer was already smiling as he recognised the Morton Grant influenced by alcohol, not the sober council painter. "How's Custer?" Andrew Fleming asked, recalling their last conversation.

Morton lifted his right hand to tap the side of his nose and winked as he replied, "Cosa Nostra" and he kept walking. Fleming chuckled to himself, "You're in the wrong country, Morton."

At precisely 3 a.m. the helicopter touched down on the dark airstrip. A single figure jumped out onto the tarmac and ran through the darkness to the dirt track where Fleming was waiting. When 'Dick' reached the car Fleming flashed his lights briefly and the helicopter lifted off.

"It's yourself, Andy." the intelligence officer remarked, recognising Fleming in the dim light of the interior lamp. "The last time I saw you was back in January."

"Aye, that's right and the weather was pretty bad. I remember." Fleming said as he pulled away onto the main road. "The roads are a bit easier to deal with now."

THE TALE OF THE OLD SCHOOL TIES

"Just as well," replied Dick, "Let me tell you about Charlie."

"Your driver in Belfast, right?" Fleming recalled.

"Yes, that Charlie. It was after I saw you last, he came to pick me up at Stormont in the armour plated buggy. I sat in the back seat so that I could spread out all my papers from that evening and the next thing I knew we were waltzing around in circles and my papers were flying everywhere. The car is doing three-sixties all the way down the road. I knew that Charlie had been on one of these ambush awareness courses and I cursed him upside down for choosing that moment to show off. Well, the car came to a halt and Charlie, well, he was chalky white. He turned to me and apologised. It was black ice."

Fleming laughed.

"I don't fancy trying to control a three ton motor car on black ice myself."

An hour later and Fleming reached the designated destination where another police car waited to continue 'Dick's' journey.

Anthony Halbrook was normally a heavy sleeper but, being alone at home, as opposed to being one of a dozen boys in a dormitory, caused him to be more alert to sounds in the night. Around three-thirty in the morning he heard the sound of a car door closing in the courtyard. After listening for further noise and hearing nothing, he looked out of his bedroom window. Anthony could see an unlit silver car parked close to the laundry room. Presumably his father was in the laundry for there was a light behind the whitewashed window. After a minute or two, the light was extinguished and the tall, lean figure of Milton Halbooth emerged from the laundry room carrying a black plastic bag in the shape of a box. After placing the bag into the boot of his car he drove off.

Anthony supposed that his father had been aware of the box and its malodorous contents. The decision had been made to dispose of it before coming into the house. Anthony went back to sleep.

When he awoke later that Sunday morning he fully expected his father to have returned home and retired to bed. There was no car and his father had not apparently returned after all. Such was the incommunicative nature of the Halbooth family that Anthony had not been entitled to expect his father or mother to be at home for his holiday return. They probably had not realised that he was due home. It was simply the way things were and the way things had always been. However, Anthony still thought it strange that his father would drive home to dispose of rotting rubbish and not enter the house.

Anthony's parents had lived life on a different level from most other people. In their intellectual academic world there was no place for sentiment or emotion, only education and the discipline to further that education. Their relationship with Anthony was more to do with biology and kindred grey matter than any familial love.

Having seen more of the normally accepted behaviour of others, as demonstrated by his fellow pupils and their talk of parents, Anthony had begun to realise that his parents were not only on a different level as parents, they were quite different as a married couple. They did not argue certainly but then they were often apart and their marriage amounted to an agreement to be connected legally, rather than any oath to remain in a loving partnership. Now in his mid-teens, Anthony Halbooth could appreciate that his choices in life were more varied than he had hitherto supposed.

On Monday morning, in complete contrast to the previous day, Anthony rose early and showered. He dressed in jeans and a checked shirt before going to the kitchen to create his own breakfast. He heard a car enter the courtyard and immediately thought of his father but it was Gretchen MacIntyre's small red car.

"So you are home, Anthony. I had heard that you were home actually." Gretchen said pleasantly as she removed her coat.

"So who told you?" Anthony asked.

"Mrs Campbell from the library. I met her at church yesterday."

"Oh I see," Anthony said, masking his disappointment. "Have you seen my father or mother recently, Gretchen?"

"No dear, I saw your dad two or three weeks ago but your mum has not been home for quite a while. I think they are having some success with their excavations.

There was something in the papers to that effect." Gretchen said in her happy, upbeat way.

"What was in the laundry room, Gretchen? Something was creating a lot of bluebottles in there." the boy asked.

The smile left Gretchen MacIntyre's face.

"I think your father must have left something in there to rot the last time he was home. The place might be locked but that is not keeping the smell or the bluebottles inside. I will have to tell him about it."

"Did he not tell you what it was?" Anthony asked.

"No. I never even knew that he had put anything in there. It was only after a few days, when your dad had gone, that I noticed the smell and the flies. I can't say that I noticed them this morning though."

"Perhaps they have all gone." Anthony said casually, not wishing to suggest any real knowledge of the matter. He left the table and returned to his room. Gretchen cleared the table and washed up. She had worked for the Halbooths long enough to know just how eccentric they were. Asking questions had a habit of providing more questions than answers, so she refrained from mentioning anything beyond the scope of her employment. Anthony was by far the most normal of the family members but he was not a typical teenager.

He reappeared in the kitchen wearing trainers and a black blouson jacket.

"I am going to the library, Gretchen. Mrs Campbell has ordered two books for me. At least one of them should be in today."

"Very good, Anthony, I will prepare a lunch for you before I go."

"That would be kind, Gretchen. Thank you."

Ten miles north of Corran Bay the ground rises slowly away from the sea. The coastal road runs north alongside the water's edge before cutting through level areas of woodland and rhododendron bushes, The motorist is constantly aware of pine forests, thousands of acres of pine forest, coating the hillside to the east of the road. Control and maintenance of this wood is the responsibility of the Forestry Commission whose track roads lead through the various sections of developing woodland.

Neil MacLean and his comrades had been together for several years in this general area of the highlands. Twenty-five years' experience and keen eyesight permitted Neil to spot any evidence of wood theft, camp fires, vehicle intrusion or damage to trees. He would be the first to admit that the size of their area did not allow the forestry men to see all that might be going on. Roads were not patrolled simply for the sake of doing so and going to and from current work sites had to substitute for surveillance.

Neil stopped his green Land Rover in an open section of stumped timber that had been cleared seven years earlier and now offered a broad daylight view over the sea.

He rolled a cigarette as he thought of his soldier son that Wednesday afternoon. The boy was due home any day from the Falklands conflict. Neil and his wife had been worried constantly through the time he had been away. He blew his cigarette smoke out of the vehicle window and looked over to the right where the landscape consisted of ghostly grey knotted trunks and stumps covered in dried out vegetation. Occasionally a red squirrel would pass through this area providing a few moments entertainment, but not today.

About thirty yards from the vehicle, Neil noticed a log that seemed to have been moved recently.

When a log has been lying on a bed of peat and heather for some time the underside of the log absorbs the moisture from the ground while the topside bleaches with the sun and wind. The distinction is obvious when the log is lifted away from the ground but the line of distinction is not visible while the log remains on the ground.

This log had been lifted for a matter of inches out of the groove that it had formed in the soft peat. This particular log was one of the larger rejects, eight inches in diameter and nine feet long but heavily knotted.

With no difficulty the forestry worker lifted the log aside and found beneath it a black plastic parcel lying along the groove, It had been partially embedded in the peat by the weight of the log but Neil was able to prise it out of the ground easily. The black wrapping was a bag, the neck of which had been gathered and secured with a cable tie. With a small sharp knife from his pocket, Neil cut the cable tie and loosened the neck of the bag apart.

THE TALE OF THE OLD SCHOOL TIES

He was immediately aware of a foul smell from within the bag. By squeezing the bag he could tell that it held something long and spongy in an unnatural way. Turning the open end of the bag towards the sun he could see the end of a bone with decaying flesh around it. He could not tell if this was human or animal remains but he would prefer that someone else tried to find out. He twisted the neck of the bag and replaced it in the groove in the ground before returning to his Land Rover and calling the office.

Thirty minutes later he was joined by Detective Sergeant Douglas Campbell and Detective Constable Darren Black.

Douglas Campbell wasted no time in telling Chief Inspector Stewart MacKellar of the package that Neil MacLean had found.

"I'm pretty sure that it's human," Campbell said with confidence. "I don't want to take the contents out of the bag. It would be better if a pathologist was the first to do that."

"Fair enough," said MacKellar. "How long has it been lying there?"

"MacLean reckons that it has been there for two or three days. After that the distinction between wet and dry wood would fade and the parcel would probably draw the attention of animals."

"Right Douglas, phone DCI Adam. Raymond Adam may have some experience of dealing with unidentified human remains. Ask him about storage for the remains. It would be better in some hospital freezer. It is not going into our fridge."

When Campbell reached the CID room he found Darren Black already speaking to Raymond Adam on the phone.

"Here's the DS now, sir."

Raymond Adam listened to the Detective Sergeant's account and considered that if this limb had been left recently then other body parts might well follow.

"I'll call Mr McLay. In the meantime, Douglas, find a fridge, or better still, a freezer for that thing."

Raymond Adam eventually submitted the severed limb to Professor Ian McLay for forensic examination. Blood and tissue samples were taken from the unclothed right arm, thought by the pathologist to have been that of a boy aged ten to twelve years of age.

Information regarding the discovery was circulated nationwide and the limb itself was in a refrigerated unit at the hospital.

Lord Lachlan Mulgrew stopped to light his pipe. With a match in his cupped hand he drew smoke repeatedly from beneath his thick grey moustache. In both hip pockets he had a flask of single malt and over his right arm hung a broken 12 bore double-barrelled shotgun. Despite his life-threatening indulgences, the laird was eighty years of age and well capable of walking for eight miles or more over the moorland of his estate. His trusted companion today, as on every day, was a black Labrador called Toby. The dog watched everything the old man did and seemed to understand every word he said.

Satisfied that his pipe was indeed lit, the laird began to stride forward again through the heather. Ahead of him lay a dirt road that traversed from left to right across the moor in a straight line providing vehicular connection between two public roads, neither of which was particularly busy. Lord Lachlan grunted to himself as he recalled the formal letter he had received several years back about this road, reminding him that it was a public right-of-way. He had always honoured the status of the scarcely used dirt track and needed no reminding from any jumped-up pompous jack-ass. He had replied to that effect in his own letter.

As he crossed the dirt road he disturbed two large crows that lifted noisily from the heather well ahead of him. He snapped the shotgun shut and loosed two shots in the direction of the crows. Toby ran off in the same direction.

"Toby, where the hell are you going? I missed the buggers." the old man rasped in frustration. He looked ahead for Toby but the dog had disappeared in the heather. "Toby, where are you?"

About fifty yards ahead of him Toby climbed up from a peat rut and began to return at walking pace with a long black object in his mouth. It was a parcel of black polythene that the dog dropped at the laird's feet, receiving his usual rub to the crown of his head in congratulation of the fetch.

"Well done, Toby," the laird said, a bit uncertain of what the dog had just brought. He knelt down beside the item which had obviously been intact in black polythene until the crows had nosily pecked holes in the plastic. The laird stuck a finger into one of the holes and pulled the plastic apart making a larger hole. There was a smell from within. The texture of the contents was soft, but the appearance of human skin was much as might be expected. It took a lot to make Lord Lachlan squeamish and he ripped the plastic further.

"Toby, old fellow, this is some poor wee lad's leg. Show me where you found it."

The Labrador bounded forward to the peat rut and stopped beside it. At the point indicated by the dog there was some disturbance of the hardened peat crust but as the laird searched along the peat bank, he found nothing more.

"Well done, Toby man, but our work is over for today old fellow. I suppose we better to get this laddie's leg back to the lodge and report this."

The discovery of a second limb in a black plastic bag had encouraged the expectation of more such parcels, the situation anticipated by DCI Adam. Mr McLay, the forensic pathologist had confirmed that the left leg, found by the laird, was consistent with the right arm found by the forestry worker, in terms of sex, age, blood group and skin tissue. There had been no old scars or remarkable features by which to narrow the scope of identification but both limbs appeared to have come from the same child.

Raymond Adam had wasted no time in preparing posters for local distribution to make the public aware of the black plastic bag discoveries and to encourage them to be alert to any such parcel. He had notified the press and the media of the recovered limbs from a dead male child. The second circulation to other police areas was again nationwide. There was no outstanding report of a missing boy in the Corran Bay area and it would not necessarily follow that subsequently found remains would be local.

TWO

The local newspaper carried the story of the body parts found among the heather and forestry. The article was no longer than a couple of paragraphs but it made farmer Archie Campbell think.

The previous year he had gone into his 'big field' to harrow and had noticed that a corner of the ploughed field had been flattened. The earth had been raised in drills just like the rest of the field but on that spot it had been flattened and there were footprints over it. At the time Archie had supposed that someone might have buried a dog or cat. He had thought at the time that somebody 'had a damn cheek' but had done no more than that. Now he wondered if that could have been something other than a dead pet. He knew that it would bother him to leave the matter unresolved now that he had thought of it. He knew just where he had seen the flattened ground even if the 'big field' was now in barley but his margins were wider this year.

With the drainage bucket attached to his 'back actor', Archie set off in the tractor for the 'big field'. If his memory served him right the spot he wanted was in the margin and not among the barley. He set the tractor on its stands and bit the bucket into ground beyond where he imagined the exact position to be. With each bucketful of earth deposited to his left, Archie jumped down to kick the soil apart. He repeated the process and found nothing within the suspected area. He elected to go deeper and after a few bucket loads he noticed a black plastic bag among the earth. He climbed down and felt the parcel, imagining that he was feeling a long bone. The parcel appeared to have shrunk inwards and Archie was no wiser as to what it was. He placed it to one side and returned to digging, finding two more parcels of similar description in close proximity to the first. Once satisfied that he had found all there was to find, he placed the three parcels aside and began to refill the hole.

The son of a neighbouring farmer stopped beside the field fence and shouted to Campbell. Archie climbed down and went to speak to the young man, telling him what he had just found and asked him to contact 'the bobbies' and get them to come out for these parcels.

Detective Chief Inspector Raymond Adam, like Detective Sergeant Douglas Campbell and Andy Fleming, had seen the television reports on the national news of the missing schoolboy William Faraday. It was the kind of case that could lead to the disposal of body parts in rural areas and the age of the victim was the same. The Faraday boy's disappearance had been at the other end of the country. Nobody would require to carry their victim such a distance before trying to hide his remains. The police in Kent would have the circulation of the discovered limbs. The dilemma was really theirs to consider.

When Raymond Adam saw the parcels found by Archie Campbell he could tell immediately that they had been wrapped in exactly the same way as the previous two; they just seemed to be older.

The pathologist agreed with him. The parts from the 'big field' were older, probably a year older, they had been wrapped in the same way and they belonged to a child of similar age. This time the parcels contained both legs and a left arm belonging to a young girl. The skeletal remains gave no further help towards identification, no old fractures, deformities or abnormalities. The pathologist guessed that dismembering had been done by means of a hacksaw and showed no particular expertise on the part of the perpetrator. The black plastic wrapping was again sent to the laboratory. Raymond Adam lifted the telephone and called Douglas Campbell.

"Dougie, a couple of things; first get that part of the field dug over again. Make sure that we are not leaving part of this poor kid in there. The other thing I want is a poster for distribution in all public places, the auction mart, the bus company, the train station, community halls, camp sites and village shops and post offices. I want people talking about this repeatedly so that there is a constant awareness of child body parts being deposited in your area. Whoever dumped these parts was not a once only visitor. They were here last year too."

Anthony Halbooth was delighted with his library book and had settled down to read immediately he had returned home that Monday.

It was now nearly two o'clock on Wednesday and he remembered that Gretchen had again said something about leaving a lunch for him. He went to the kitchen and found a prepared tray in the fridge. He made himself a mug of tea and went back upstairs to his room. He switched on the small radio beside his bed as he ate and looked out of the window. Every hour on the hour there was a brief version of the main news. The disappearance of a young boy from Letherford School in Kent was reported. The broadcast had obviously been on before and concern for the boy was mounting.

Anthony switched off the radio and thought about that school name, Letherford. He had heard of Letherford School in Kent. He had heard that same school being mentioned in conversations between his parents three or four years earlier. Had they considered placing him there? He had not really paid much attention to the matter at the time but Letherford School had certainly been spoken about. He drank his tea and resumed his reading.

When Archie Campbell was told that his parcels had indeed contained more body parts from a child he was more than agreeable to a more thorough search. He took Dougie Campbell and Darren Black to the 'big field' and provided a square demarcation which exceeded his memory of the manually dug area of the previous year.

"If it's no in that square then it's no there at all." Archie declared.

"Fair enough, Archie, we'll get some help and get on with it. I suppose it will have to be hand dug to be sure of checking every bit of it properly. How deep down were these parcels you found?"

"About three or four feet down, maybe," Archie said after some thought. "They were deep enough for my plough to go clean over them, that's for sure."

"Great," Dougie said with resignation as he surveyed the nine yards by nine yards square plot.

Six hours later, with the assistance of two village constables, Dougie and Darren were satisfied that they had searched every drop of earth from the hole. The floor of the hole was now dense clay that defied penetration by mortal man and garden spade.

"I'll put that lot back wi' the tractor if you're satisfied." Archie volunteered.

Two hundred miles to the north-east of Corran Bay, in a secluded clearing close to a burn of clear water, there was an even more precise excavation taking place.

Penelope Halbooth and her team were uncovering a sunken community dwelling within a perimeter wall. The local natural stone was a grained rock which broke naturally into slabs of stone, ideal for building. There was a striking resemblance in what they were finding, to the subterranean dwellings found in Orkney. Although this Sutherland village was less distinct due to water erosion, it was no older than Skara Brae in Orkney and may even have been constructed at a later time by tribes or families migrating south.

The team members were working every daylight hour, scraping, digging and brushing their way to a clearer realisation of the ancient habitat. Each significant find, no matter how small, had been documented, photographed and stored. Among the team, the conversations and considerations had been confined to the dig, reflecting an enthusiasm and excitement akin to children in a sweet shop. At night the archaeologists retired to large tents behind the dig site.

Responsibility for cooking meals and collecting supplies was a duty that rotated around the female members of the team and involved trips to Brora or Helmsdale. The domestic scene, cooking and shopping included, were foreign to Penelope's mental habitat and as practical duties really tested her abilities. She had to accept that her participation was a necessary part of the mission and a price she had to pay.

It actually hurt her emotionally to be driving away from the dig site, heading for town with a shopping list. After several minutes of being alone in the car and remote from her own piece of history, her thoughts drifted to present day. That was an irony. What day was that exactly? Which month was it? She had to admit that she had lost track and did not really know.

The items listed represented the essential needs of a dozen people for a week at least. Life at the camp was not about consumption, in fact, their existence was frugal, but the trolley filled up just the same. As she waited impatiently behind an elderly lady at the single check-out, Penelope looked around her and her eyes fell on a newspaper stand. No-one at the camp had asked for a newspaper, no-one ever did. Nevertheless, she stared at the newspaper headline that read, 'Letherford: Foul play suspected'. She stepped across and lifted the newspaper. She had not purchased a newspaper in years but she must have this one. Was that really the date?

Anthony Halbooth was lying on his bed, reading Horace, when the phone rang. He ran downstairs and eagerly picked up the handset, "Hello?"

"Is that you Anthony? So you are home. Where is your father?"

"I have no idea, mother. He has not set foot in the house since I came home and Gretchen has not seen him for two or three weeks."

"This is not good, Anthony. I will call again next week, probably on the same day. If your father arrives home you might tell him that, will you?"

THE TALE OF THE OLD SCHOOL TIES

"Yes, mother, I'll tell him."

She had already rung off.

What had she been concerned about? He replaced the handset slowly. With either of his parents, heightened concern was a thing of the moment and could as easily relate to a world war breaking out, as it could to the fridge door being left open. His mother was not given to phoning home from an excavation, not until it was over. Father's whereabouts were never uppermost in her mind and she had made no enquiry about her only son, recently returned from another school year. Anthony shook his head and returned to Horace.

"What do you mean, 'simply disappeared'?" Gerald Faraday ranted in frustration. His wife Marylin was standing beside him with her hands tightly clasped and her lips quivering. "There are a thousand boys at that school, how could he simply disappear, as you put it?"

John Wetherby looked patiently at Faraday. The school roll was much less than a thousand but this was no time to be correcting the point.

"Everyone was leaving over the course of the day, with the exception of a few, including William, who intended to stay a little longer. That did not make William subject to detention. There was no reason for him not to leave the school grounds any more than any other Saturday. He had told his friends in the dormitory that he hoped to buy a maths set and for that purpose he would be going into town, which town he never actually said. A boy in school uniform leaving the school grounds on that day would not be remembered by any person who thought it unusual, whether or not they knew him. I believe the police are making enquiries to trace everyone who does know William and who may have seen him."

"It has been five days now, Mr Wetherby, do the police think that William will be all right?" Marylin Faraday whimpered in a voice that begged for consolation.

"I have no information from the police, I am afraid, Mrs Faraday. They tend to ask questions without divulging answers, but I know that they will want to speak to you both. That would afford you the opportunity to enquire directly. I am sure that they would expect that and you may well be entitled to information that they would not be giving to me."

"Who is in charge of the police investigation?" Gerald Faraday asked bluntly with some hint of his adopted accent.

"A Detective Superintendent Barrowman came to see me." Wetherby replied. "James Barrowman, I think he must be the person in charge. I have his telephone number on a card. Yes, here it is. I'll take a note of his number for my own use and then you can have it."

Lying on his bed with an apple in one hand and a book on Augustus in the other, Anthony Halbooth read with a greater appetite than he ate. He wanted to be able to finish his library books by tomorrow, Friday. He had an irritating desire to actively enquire into the enigma that his parents represented. A year ago it would have been unthinkable to question his parents and their strange attitudes and behaviour, but his own development was now demanding a proper understanding. He would speak with Gretchen tomorrow.

The Faradays had caught up with James Barrowman. The Detective Superintendent welcomed them into a comfortable room of carpet and soft chairs, designed to give no impression of being an interview room but intended for the interviewing of persons beset by trauma.

The police officer first enquired about the relationship between the couple and their son. He enquired as to occupations and other family members. Was there a past connection with the school? How had William felt about attending the school? Had he made enemies or friends? Had he interests outside the school? Had he relatives to whom he might have gone? Were they aware of the identification tags on school uniform? Yes they were. Marylin Faraday had sown her son's name tags onto his clothing personally.

When all the background had been covered and it had been established that the parents had been on the other side of the world when William had gone missing, Barrowman turned to the more difficult part of the interview.

"We still have not found William but we do have some of his school uniform discarded in a waste bin. The items have his name tags on them."

The Detective Superintendent paused to allow this information to sink in. He intentionally omitted the fact that the clothing had been blood-stained. The Faradays looked at each other in shock. Their son would never have discarded his school uniform into a litter bin of his own accord.

"Someone has taken him," Marylin Faraday said, her hands rising to her forehead. She began to weep and her husband placed an arm around her shoulders.

"That is as much as we can tell you at this time," Barrowman said softly. "There may well be further developments and any breakthrough could lead to a succession of events. I would need a contact number and an address for you. I would certainly hope to keep you in the picture as events unfold. In the meantime I would ask you to pay more attention to the facts that I may provide rather than any speculation from the press for public consumption."

Anthony Halbooth had finished his book on Augustus and now dared to enter his father's study to look through the drawers and box files. There were document files, lecture notes, case studies and all manner of correspondence scattered around the room with no apparent order as to where each item deserved to be. The lecture notes and study papers might have interested Anthony at another time but today was about seeking out the unexpected and eventually he found it.

There, among loose letters kept in a drawer, was a reply from the Board of Trustees at Letherford School, Kent. Milton Halbooth had seemingly applied for a position as head of the science department at the school, making the point in his application that his father had been a pupil there. This letter had been received ten years ago and the board had rejected his application. Knowing his father's nature, that of a proud man, Anthony would not expect that this news would have been well received. His father would more likely have been extremely angry.

Anthony also came across documents of headed paper concerning his father's current employers, an international pharmaceutical company. He took some of these papers and the rejection letter from Letherford, folded them and placed them in the inside pocket of his jacket.

When Gretchen MacIntyre arrived for work the following morning, she found Anthony sitting in the kitchen, his library books on the table in front of him. He looked thoughtful and a bit despondent but with Anthony, or any other Halbooth, it was difficult to be sure. Gretchen made tea for them both.

"Gretchen, do you use these shiny black bags?" Anthony asked.

"Yes, Anthony I have them for the kitchen bin." She

opened a cupboard door and pointed. "See, there they are."

"Have you given any to father at any time?" he asked.

"No dear," Gretchen laughed as she spoke. "I can't really imagine him asking for any."

Anthony smiled. He knew what she meant, his father was not the tidying kind.

"Are you going back to the library today?" Gretchen asked, nodding towards his books.

"Yes, I will take them back but I doubt that I will get new ones yet, not until Mrs Campbell has had time to order them."

The tea was finished and Anthony rose from the table and lifted his books.

"I will go now, Gretchen, take care."

"Goodbye Anthony," Gretchen said quietly. A strange feeling crept over her. There was a habitual orderliness to Anthony Halbooth. Only when he was leaving to return to school did he ever use the phrase, 'Goodbye, take care'. Short term departures would normally amount to a wave of the hand and a 'Bye'.

Andrew Fleming was standing in the library talking to Mrs Campbell when Anthony came in. Fleming was holding a wad of posters, the recent version designed in response to Raymond Adam's wishes. He had already posted one of the posters on the public notice board, covering the previous poster. As Anthony Halbooth

THE TALE OF THE OLD SCHOOL TIES

entered and saw the police officer with Mrs Campbell, he stopped and looked at the public notice board, his natural shyness discouraging the notion of approaching the librarian while she was speaking to a policeman. On the notice board he saw the poster telling the public of the more recent discovery of child body parts in the area and asking for public vigilance in reporting any unusual parcels of black plastic in out of the way places. Mrs Campbell had whispered to Fleming that the young customer was shy and Fleming took the hint. He went to the far side of the enclosed desk and Mrs Campbell returned to her console behind the desk. Only then did Anthony come forward to return his books.

"You were not long with these, Anthony." Mrs Campbell commented to the boy with her usual pleasant smile.

"I spent time on the Horace odes but there was not a lot about Mycaenas in the Augustus book." Anthony explained.

Fleming heard what was said and as Mrs Campbell placed the book on Horace aside Fleming picked it up and began to read the cover page.

"Will you be needing more, Anthony?" Mrs Campbell asked, aware that the books might well have to be ordered.

"Yes, but not today, Mrs Campbell, thank you. Do you have photo-copying facilities here?" Anthony asked, his eyes glancing towards Fleming as he spoke. Fleming ignored him and kept reading.

"Yes, Anthony, over in the corner there is a machine. I will have to charge ten pence per copy, I'm afraid. They check the meter against my little book, you see."

"Oh, that's all right. I would expect to pay, thank you." Anthony replied.

He looked purposefully at Andrew Fleming as he passed the police officer, still reading. Fleming ignored the boy but winked at Mrs Campbell once the young boy has passed. Anthony looked at Fleming again as he returned from the machine.

"How many?" Mrs Campbell asked pleasantly.

"Six copies, Mrs Campbell. Here is your sixty pence, thank you. I will give you sufficient notice if I decide on further books."

"Thank you, Anthony, three days is normally ample time. Here is a plastic pocket for your papers. I don't need it."

The boy thanked Mrs Campbell and she smiled after him as he headed for the door, glancing at the police poster as he left.

"Strange." Mrs Campbell remarked.

"What is strange?" Fleming asked.

"That is young Anthony Halbooth. Normally he takes out books all through his school holidays without interruption, but not this time apparently."

"Maybe going away with his folks." Fleming suggested.

"I would doubt that." Mrs Campbell replied. "Anyway, he's not the only one acting strangely about here. When did you start reading Horace?"

THE TALE OF THE OLD SCHOOL TIES

Fleming laughed. "Well, I have a lawyer friend who keeps quoting Horace to me and expects me to understand what he's talking about. That's why I lifted the book but it's actually not bad, if you stick to the English pages at the back."

"So you want to take it out?" Mrs Campbell asked cheekily.

"Not just now, thank you."

"That young man had a good look at you." Mrs Campbell said. "And I am pretty sure he took note of your shoulder number."

"He won't be the first to do that." Fleming said. "I better get the rest of these posters delivered. 'Tempus fugit' as Horace might have said."

The following Monday morning saw puzzled expressions on the faces of Gretchen McIntyre, Raymond Adam and James Barrowman.

Gretchen McIntyre arrived at the lodge house to find that Anthony Halbooth was not there. She had made the boys' bed after speaking to him on Friday morning and it appeared not to have been slept in since. There were no dirty dishes and the refrigerator contents remained the same. The toothpaste and toothbrush were missing from the bathroom. Gretchen was not in a position to know that Anthony's passport and his passbook for his building society account were also gone, but she knew that Anthony was unaccounted for. There was no way of contacting

Anthony's mother and his father's telephone was a London business number. She rang the London number and enquired if Professor Halbooth was available. The receptionist at the drug company was able to tell her that Milton Halbooth was out of the country. Gretchen explained the situation to the girl and asked that he be informed if possible. In the meantime, she would take the girl's advice and call the police.

Raymond Adam looked over the pathology report on the arm and two legs, recently discovered in the farmer's field, but older since their time of death, than the previous discoveries. Again, dismembering had been performed by means of a hacksaw without any indication of surgical skill. This was pretty much what Adam had expected. The laboratory examination of the bag that had contained the female victim's arm was more interesting. Among the stickiness of long congealed blood there were fibres. These fibres had been segregated and consisted, in differing lengths, of two main colours, consistent in their thickness and microscopic appearance. The colours were mid-grey and a deep rose pink. There had been no material of any kind found in the bag other than these fibres and it was believed from their location on the inner surface that they had transferred from the sawn upper end of the arm to the inner surface of the plastic bag by contact. Raymond Adam could imagine the freshly severed arm lying on the carpet, perhaps in the car boot, before being placed into the black bag for eventual disposal.

THE TALE OF THE OLD SCHOOL TIES

James Barrowman had obtained CCTV tapes from service stations and public locations between the school and the service station where the clothing had been found. Different officers had scanned the tapes around the clock and found no trace of anyone answering the description of William J. Faraday. Every instance of persons from vehicles depositing rubbish into bins had been catalogued and the tapes had been retained but nothing had suggested criminal activity or secrecy. The physical searches around the area of the school had failed to locate any human remains. He could recall how, the previous year, the CID in Surrey had been in contact after their schoolgirl had been reported missing from the Mary Upton School for Girls. That case had similar features to the missing boy form Letherford in 1980, Richard Barton. Neither Richard Barton nor Helen Holloway had been found, but how much had Surrey learned? He would ring them.

Andrew Fleming wasted no time in responding to the call from Gretchen McIntyre. He recognised the name immediately and recalled the young student at the library. When he arrived at the secluded lodge he found Gretchen in an anxious state.

"When did you last see him?" Fleming asked.

"Friday morning, he went to the library and it looks like he never came back." Gretchen said.

"I just knew something was wrong."

"You knew on Friday?" Fleming asked. "What was wrong on Friday?"

"Something was bothering him. He was down. He doesn't say all that much but he was depressed. He said 'goodbye' when he was going to the library but it sounded more like a real 'goodbye', you know what I mean?"

"First things first, Gretchen, can we check the house, just to be completely sure that he is not in here?"

"Sure, we do that together, yes?"

"Absolutely, now let's start with his bedroom."

Gretchen McIntyre led Fleming upstairs to the single bedroom overlooking the courtyard. The bed was tidy and Fleming checked beneath it. There was only the small case that Anthony had brought home from school. The police officer pulled it out and opened it.

"Anthony is too big to be in there." Gretchen observed.

Fleming smiled.

"I know that. I also know that Anthony is a very clever guy. If he wanted to leave a note or a clue as to what he was doing or where he was going, he might put it in something like this. Is there another bag, Gretchen, one that he could use to take things with him?"

"There was a backpack usually in this cupboard."

She opened the full height cupboard behind the door and over the stairwell. Fleming could see hundreds of books on shelves but Gretchen bent down to the floor and looked for the bag she had mentioned.

"It is gone." she said with certainty. "It was there last week."

They both looked around the room in the hope of

THE TALE OF THE OLD SCHOOL TIES

seeing the backpack but it was not there. Fleming noticed the absence of anything associated with music. There were no compact discs, no records, tapes, instruments or devices for playing music. This was unusual in a teenager's room. There was no television either, just the bedside clock/radio. He looked up at the fairly high ceiling and saw a hand-written poster there, Gretchen followed his gaze.

"That is different. For years he has had a poster that said, 'No Pain, No Gain'. It was still there on Friday morning. Now it has been replaced with this."

Fleming could see that the poster was hand-written in Latin.

"Is there something to stand on, Gretchen? I would like to see that notice properly."

"Use the steps from his father's room. I'll fetch them. I'm sure that is what Anthony would have used."

Gretchen returned with a set of wooden steps and Fleming could easily reach the notice pinned to the ceiling on top of the old poster. The top of the new notice had been doubled back. On that hidden section was written, 'ad pater'. Beneath that Anthony had printed 'AMICUS PLATO SED MAGIS AMICA VERITAS'.

Fleming copied this writing in his notebook and asked Gretchen if she understood it. She shook her head and he laughed. "That makes two of us." He replaced the poster just as it had been. "I told you he might leave a note."

The pair moved on to the other rooms and ensured that

every cupboard or space where a body could hide or be hidden was checked for the presence of Anthony. Fleming made no comment on the separate bedrooms of the parents. Each of the bedrooms had a section devoted to a desk, cabinets and bookcases. Professor Halbooth's bedroom devoted to material on bio-chemistry, his wife's to archaeology. The bathroom was still equipped as it might have been sixty years earlier with a free-standing, unboxed metal bath with huge taps and an enclosed plunger/stopper. The large hand-basin was supported by a wrought iron arrangement, similar to the old pre-electric sewing machines. Above it was a white, modern bathroom cupboard with door mirror. Gretchen opened it to show that Anthony had taken his toothbrush and toothpaste. Fleming nodded.

"This is all there is to see upstairs." Gretchen explained. "There is no real attic because of the coombe ceilings."

She led Fleming downstairs and into the small lounge. The room was dark, probably caused by the partially clad walls and the dark, heavy drapes. The sofa and two armchairs were winged and armed with loose covers in a varied but time-faded floral pattern. Fleming walked around the furniture, to see the areas behind chairs and curtains, before opening the door in the corner. It was another cupboard of shelves stacked neatly, but randomly, with tinned foodstuffs, stationery, torches and light bulbs. There was no space for Anthony.

"Then there is this small room." said Gretchen, walking

THE TALE OF THE OLD SCHOOL TIES

into an equally small room with a centre table and chairs. A bay window looked out to a walled garden of modest proportions. Fleming noticed the small garden shed and in the corner of the garden, an incinerator.

"Is that incinerator ever used, Gretchen?"

"I think sometimes for rubbish." she replied. "The Professor burns things in it, paper mostly, then the wind comes and makes a terrible mess."

"And the shed?" Fleming asked.

"It has an old lawnmower and shears, spade, fork, rake. There is only one key, always in the lock." she explained with a smile.

Fleming looked at the only other furniture in this room, a display cabinet of glasses and plates looking dated but remarkably clean.

"You clean this, don't you, Gretchen?"

"I clean everything, Andrew. It is a good job that the Halbooths are away as much as they are. Cleaning is not easy when they are here, any one of them."

Fleming was looking at a framed photograph on top of the display. It was the only photograph in the house other than a group photograph of archaeologists in Penelope's bedroom. This picture showed a young Professor Halbooth and his wife, Penelope, holding a two year old Anthony. The family were standing in front of a dark green Morris Traveller in magnificent condition for its age.

"Look at that car, Gretchen, I can remember those."

"I can remember that one." Gretchen said pointedly.

"The professor only sold it about two years ago and it was still in great condition."

"Why did he sell it?" Fleming wondered.

"A friend of his, another scientist, wanted it and the professor was finding it heavy on petrol. He goes to Glasgow or Edinburgh and flies from there but even so the old car was not economical, so he sold it."

They both heard a car pull up outside in the courtyard and the wooden back door of the house was thrown open as a small, slightly built woman of forty plus burst through to the room where Gretchen and Fleming stood.

"What are the police doing here, in my house? What is wrong? Where is Milton? Where is Anthony? Gretchen, explain yourself."

"Anthony is missing, Doctor Halbooth." Gretchen began. "He has been gone since Friday."

"He was here on Thursday, I spoke to him." Penelope Halbooth stated as if disputing the disappearance.

"He was also here on Friday." Fleming said emphatically. "But not since."

This woman was a bag of nervous energy but her mind seemed too active to think straight.

"So where did he go? Are you here for Anthony? You are not here for Milton?" she seemed to find it inconceivable that the police officer was interested in her son and not her husband.

"Your husband is not missing, as far as I know, Doctor Halbooth. He seems not to have been here since Anthony came home from school."

THE TALE OF THE OLD SCHOOL TIES

"He is a very busy man, my husband. He travels the world, you know." she was still speaking quickly but was looking less frantic.

"So I understand. Where is he just now? Do you know?" Fleming asked without suggestion.

"I have no idea. He could be in Pennsylvania or he could be in prison. I have been very busy too, you see."

"Yes, of course." Fleming conceded, recalling all that had been said of the Halbooths. "I was simply checking around the house with Gretchen to ensure that Anthony was not here."

"He is not here. I can just feel it." the archaeologist stated.

"Nevertheless we have only the kitchen and these outhouses to check and then we are done." Fleming asserted. He nodded to Gretchen and they headed into the kitchen. Gretchen opened each of the cupboards in turn and Fleming noticed again just how clean and orderly things were. "You work hard in here, Gretchen." he said, knowing that his praise would fall on the ears of Penelope Halbooth. He also noticed the black plastic bags stacked in one of the cupboards.

"Now there is just the garage and the workshop." Gretchen said as she opened the rear door to the courtyard. "We cannot get into the laundry room. The professor has the only key."

"What is in the laundry room, Gretchen? Have you ever seen in there?"

"Yes. I have been in there with Professor Halbooth. There is a solid wood table, a stone sink and an old mangle. He doesn't really use it, the place is either freezing cold or very hot. The sun shines through the skylight, you see."

Fleming was nodding. They entered the garage which was part of the same long building and was apparently unlocked, in fact, there was no lock. Shelves had been erected singly on the stone walls and old paint tins sat beside old tools on these shelves, tied to the wall by cobwebs. Against the rear wall there stood a chest freezer with a cable leading up the wall and into the adjoining room. Fleming had a quick look in the freezer. There were a few packages of meat and fish. Gretchen shook her head as they looked around.

"They never use this place now."

"And the workshop?" Fleming prompted.

"Between this and the laundry, come on." Gretchen said with some show of reluctance that Fleming put down to the appearance of Mrs Halbooth. Once Fleming had driven away, Gretchen would be left in her 'interesting' company.

The workshop was similar to the garage but there were benches and tools around the four walls and a table-saw in the centre of the floor. Fleming saw the cable from the freezer in the garage. It entered the workshop at ceiling height and went into the nearest socket.

"Is there electricity in the laundry room, Gretchen?" he asked.

"Only for light, same as the garage." she replied.

Fleming nodded and went for a quick look into the garden shed.

"I will need all Anthony's particulars, you know, his age, date of birth, school, relatives addresses, banking details if there are any and any recent photographs. Can you help with any of these, before I ask Mrs Halbooth?"

"Oh, don't call her Mrs Halbooth," Gretchen advised. "Stick with 'Doctor' if you want her to tell you anything. She won't have any recent photograph of Anthony but I have some, taken at the Christmas break. His folks weren't here you see, I invited him along to have Christmas dinner with us. I took some shots then. They are at home but I'll get them for you. He has a building society account, that one in town next to the woollen shop. I'll listen to what his mother tells you and if I can fill in any gaps then I will." Gretchen promised.

"That sounds like a plan." Fleming said with a smile.

After a difficult twenty minutes of questions in both directions and explanations to accompany each answer, Fleming left with enough information to complete an initial Missing Person report in respect of Anthony Halbooth.

THREE

When James Barrowman spoke to the CID in Surrey he learned that they had just received news of a possible development in the case of the missing girl, Helen Holloway. The police in Strathclyde, Scotland had circulated their discovery of human remains matching a girl of Helen's age. Furthermore, there had been forensic identification of fibres within the plastic wrapping as being of mid-grey and rose pink colours. These were the school uniform colours of the Mary Upton School for Girls. Like William Faraday and Richard Barton, Helen Holloway had been wearing school uniform at the time of her disappearance, the last day of summer term the previous year, 1981. What was also significant was that only three limbs had been found in one location. Helen's right arm, head and torso were still to be found. It was a matter of record that her right arm had been contained in a plaster cast, a plaster cast signed by her friends from school, following a sporting accident. This could explain, perhaps, why the right arm would have been discarded separately. Barrowman was reminded that body parts had been found in that same area for a boy of William's age.

Barrowman knew this. He also knew he could expect no coloured fibres from these body parts.

He was encouraged enough to call DCI Raymond Adam.

"So you actually have two outstanding 'Missing Persons' from your school?" Raymond Adam confirmed. Both boys apparently taken on the last day of term just like the Surrey girl, but the year before her disappearance and the year after? I think the body parts may be up here but the motive seems to be very much at your end, Jim. Are these two schools connected in any way?"

"Not in any obvious way, Raymond, but I see what you are getting at, why these two schools? We have recovered the limbs but still have no real identification, something the killer seems to have considered. I think the heads will not be easily found, or the girl's right arm with a known fracture."

Raymond Adam explained the type of terrain where the parcels had been found and explained the measures he had taken to maintain public awareness and vigilance.

"I think it is only a matter of time before we have a breakthrough, Jim. The most important development is that we know of each other's enquiry."

Andrew Fleming had gone to the library and consulted a Latin dictionary, ignoring his past difficulties with the language. Even with the benefit of the dictionary he could not be certain of the meaning of Anthony's self-penned poster. Mrs Campbell recommended Mr George Henderson, the Latin teacher at the local high school. Mr Henderson was apparently a real gentleman and would be happy to assist. Together the librarian and the police officer looked up Mr Henderson's telephone number. Fleming would call him that evening.

"Oh, I see, Mr Fleming. I will be glad to help you. What is the quote, I will write it down?" Henderson said confidently.

Andrew Fleming read the text slowly, spelling each word, to allow the teacher to write it down accurately.

"Thank you, Mr Fleming. I think this is from Aristotle, a contemporary, or rather a pupil, of Plato. He would have looked on Plato as a father figure. It will be translated slightly differently by modern scholars but the meaning is essentially, 'Plato is dear to me, but the truth is dearer still'. Does that provide any significance to you?"

"Yes, I believe it does amount to a message from Anthony and coming from a recent state of mind prior to disappearing. He saw me looking at a classics book and he might be assuming that I can understand messages like this." Fleming said, wishing he had not picked up that library book.

"And he was wrong?" Mr Henderson supposed. "Never mind, Mr Fleming, you can feel free to consult me if you need further help. I hope the boy turns up."

The following morning Fleming spoke to Dougie

Campbell about the body parts enquiry and heard of the interest from Kent and Surrey. Their conversation was interrupted by Chief Inspector McKellar who entered the room to pass Fleming another small white envelope. He invited Campbell to come to his office to discuss the missing children enquiry but stopped at the door to look back at Andrew Fleming who had opened the envelope to read the brief note within, 'Dick – outward – 1a.m.'.

"All right, Andrew?"

"All right, sir."

Anthony Halbooth had taken the train to Glasgow and then he began an overnight bus journey from Glasgow to London. He had taken breakfast in a small cafeteria and used their washroom to 'freshen up'. Then began his long walk across town, frequently stopping to ask for directions, he eventually reached the offices of Ola-Plage, the large international drug company that employed his father.

The front of the building was all glass, reflecting the image of other buildings and the sun's rays. To Anthony it also looked a bit daunting. Through the glass he could see the huge reception desk behind which sat three receptionists in company livery. A notice directed all visitors to report to these ladies. Beyond the desk stood a security guard and beyond him a series of lifts. Anthony finally ventured inside having deduced that there would never be a lull in the steady flow of people coming and going.

"I am Anthony Halbooth. Could I speak to my father,

Professor Milton Halbooth, please?" he asked the girl nearest the door.

"Do you have identification, sir?" she asked in a well-practiced way.

"Only my bank book." Anthony replied as he struggled to remove the blue passbook from his jacket pocket. The girl looked at him sympathetically and patiently waited to check the name on the passbook.

"Your father is out of the country, Anthony. Would you like to speak to his secretary?"

Anthony gave it some thought.

"Yes, I think she might help."

"I will just check to see if she is available."

The receptionist rang through to an extension and explained the young visitor.

When she had rung off the receptionist stood up and leaned forward towards Anthony.

"Here is a 'Visitor' badge, Anthony. You must wear this on the front of your jacket during your visit and return it to me when you are leaving." She pinned the badge in place. "Now go along to the lifts and take one to the fourth floor. Go to your left through two fire-doors and the second office on your right is Mrs Moreno. She is your dad's secretary."

Anthony thanked the girl and followed the directions. When he knocked on the office door it was opened by a smart looking lady in her forties. She introduced herself as Mrs Moreno and said it was a pleasure to meet Anthony

THE TALE OF THE OLD SCHOOL TIES

at last, although in truth she had not known that the boy existed prior to Gretchen's telephone call.

Anthony asked Mrs Moreno how long his father had been out of the country. She told him that the Professor had been in the United States at different locations for the past month.

"You mean he was not back here last weekend?" the boy objected.

"Oh now that you mention it," Mrs Moreno said, reaching for a large desk diary. "He did have a speaking engagement with a London Commerce group on the Saturday afternoon. He spoke about it on the phone during last week, so he had remembered. He must have flown back for that, so he would be in this country at the weekend, as you say, I just never saw him."

"In the past month have there been other occasions when he would have had to return briefly like that?" Anthony asked, making Mrs Moreno raise her eyebrows at the audacity of the question.

With a show of reluctance and reservation she flicked through the diary and mentioned each location and venue, each date involved.

"No. Everything else was in America. He was only home last Saturday as far as his schedule shows. You are on school holidays now in Scotland, aren't you. You will be wondering when you might see your dad again. Well, it looks as if he will be back from America in the week of 19 July. I would imagine that he will be home that week." Mrs Moreno said with a smile.

"Have you always been my father's secretary, Mrs Moreno?" Anthony asked formally.

"Since your father came to Ola-Plage ten years ago, yes," she answered.

"Well, it has been a pleasure to meet you, Mrs Moreno. You have been a great help, thank you."

"You are very welcome, Anthony. You have come such a long way. Are you intending to visit other places in London?"

Anthony smiled as he realised that Mrs Moreno had visions of him going around the museums or the zoo. They were both heading for the door.

"I certainly intend to visit elsewhere." he said positively. "I must make my trip worthwhile, as you suggest. Goodbye and thank you for seeing me."

Mrs Moreno returned to her desk a little uncertain about the purpose of Anthony's visit. She consoled herself with a reminder that he was a Halbooth after all.

Anthony was equally mystified. His father had been in a position to make a quick visit to Corran bay during the night of Saturday into Sunday before returning to America but he had been in the States when the schoolboy had gone missing. However, Anthony would follow his other plan and go to Letherford School.

The duty of conveying the military intelligence officer could be awkward domestically, as it was invariably a night exercise, even when Fleming was dayshift or day off.

He was the only locally trained officer in 'close protection duty' and that meant that the job was always his. When he was on holiday the officer from the neighbouring area would carry out the complete journey with Fleming doing the same when his counterpart was on holiday. It was essential that Dick knew who to identify and trust.

Shortly before 1 a.m. Fleming returned to the lay-by where he had last seen Dick and parked there without lights. Right on time the lay-by was lit up by the headlights of the other patrol car which had its lights extinguished as it stopped. Dick ran from the other car and joined Fleming for the final leg of his road journey.

"It must be tiring for you, Dick, all this car transferring business every time." Fleming commented. When there was no immediate response he chuckled. "I don't want to know where you go or how far you have to travel, my only point is how tiring it must be." He could imagine Dick smiling in the darkness.

"Yes, of course, Andy, home for me is a long way, even if I was permitted a direct route."

"You have security at home, too?" Fleming asked.

"Yes, it is as much for my home as it is for me, so I can't complain. It seems that our schoolchildren are not even safe nowadays."

"You refer to the missing boy from Letherford?" Fleming said.

"Yes, I suppose you heard about it up here?" Dick suggested.

"It was on the national news." Fleming replied.

"Of course, it's a desperately poor business that, things were safer in my day."

"You went to Letherford?" Fleming asked spontaneously. It had been something in the way Dick had spoken of Letherford that prompted the question.

"I did, Andy, although I am not supposed to tell you things like that."

"Don't worry, Dick, 'things like that' won't be raised again unless we choose to mention it. There may be a connection between the missing schoolchildren and this area. We have been turning up body parts from children recently. Are there any former pupils or staff from Letherford in this area, do you know?"

"Not that I know of, Andy, but I have lost track of most people that I knew back then and the staff has probably changed too. Have you any particular person in mind?"

"There are no 'names in the frame' as they speak about, Dick, but I only know one possible former pupil, Milton Halbooth, a drugs professor."

"I have heard of him, Andy, but he never went to Letherford when I was there. It didn't hold him back at Oxford though."

Dick was looking pensively at Fleming and without looking back, Fleming could tell.

The Intelligence Officer took a small white card from his breast pocket and handed it to Fleming.

THE TALE OF THE OLD SCHOOL TIES

"Take this card, Andy and call me if you think I can help with your enquiry. Just don't give the card to anyone else or call me when there is someone else present."

Fleming took the card and put it in his own breast pocket.

"Thanks, I know the drill." he said.

"You could always come over to Ulster for a spell, Andy. I am sure I could set it up if you want." Dick offered.

"I've been already, Dick. Once is enough." Fleming said positively, aware that Dick would suspect that he was simply refusing under pretext. "Give my regards to Freddie Frayne if you see him."

"I will." Dick promised. Now he knew where Andy had been.

They arrived at the airstrip and Fleming switched off the car lights. He opened the car window a little and heard the unmistakable sound of rotor blades.

"Your boys are here, Dick. There are no silent approaches among these hills."

Two minutes later the Intelligence Officer was aboard the dark helicopter rising into the dark sky.

The following morning Anthony Halbooth came face to face with John Wetherby. Young Anthony had simply walked through the front door of the main school building and asked the man descending the staircase if he could see the headmaster.

John Wetherby took his young visitor to his office and asked what he could do for him.

"You see, sir, my father applied for a position here at this school ten years ago. I have a copy of the letter he received, turning him down for the post." Anthony passed the copy letter across to Wetherby.

"Oh, I see, a Head of Science appointment. Your father must have made the short list. Is he a scientist or a teacher, your father?"

"He is a professor in biochemistry." Anthony replied. "It doesn't say there why he was turned down." The boy sounded critical of the letter.

"No, it doesn't. Is that what you want to know? Why he wasn't appointed?" Wetherby asked.

"Yes. I want to know how he might have felt about being turned down." Anthony said.

"Has he not told you himself?"

"No, but he wouldn't tell me anyway, regardless of his feelings."

John Wetherby wondered why this young man should be asking about such a matter ten years after it occurred. Had his father committed suicide over the affair? Or had he simply died in the interim? Perhaps the reasons would become clear.

"I will see what I can learn from my files although the actual appointment would have been decided by the Board of Trustees. I will look at what I know about the successful candidate, our present Head of Science."

THE TALE OF THE OLD SCHOOL TIES

He crossed the room to a filing cabinet, took out a file and returned to his desk. After glancing over the first pages he looked up at Anthony.

"This tells me that the successful candidate was chosen from a most impressive short list that included a pharmaceutical biochemist, probably your dad, a marine biologist and two research chemists. The man who got the position was a former head of science at another school and it was that teaching background that swayed the decision over four excellent applicants. Does that answer your question Anthony?"

"Yes sir, it does, but I have another question. Was my father ever a pupil of this school?"

John Wetherby looked again at this file before choosing a CD from a drawer and inserting it into his computer.

"Milton Halbooth, now let us see. This should let us know pretty quickly." he said as he watched the monitor. "There we have it, no, your father was not a pupil at Letherford, although there was once a Josiah Halbooth, your grandfather perhaps. Is there anything else?"

"No sir. That was all I wanted to know." Anthony said, rising from his chair. "Has the missing boy been found yet?"

"No, I'm afraid not. Did you know him?"

Anthony shook his head.

"No. I heard about him on the radio news. Thank you, Mr Wetherby."

Watching him leave, John Wetherby lifted the telephone

and dialled the number he had recently scribbled on his notepad.

That same morning at Corran Bay, Gretchen MacIntyre brought Fleming the photographs of Anthony Halbooth, taken at her own home the previous Christmas. They were good photographs but Fleming wondered how many people would recognise Anthony Halbooth with a smile on his face.

"Has anything happened to Anthony since he came home from school, Gretchen, anything to occupy his mind and take him away from his studies? Perhaps something he couldn't understand." Fleming asked.

The housekeeper thought carefully. "The bluebottles, maybe. It's something I don't understand myself, actually."

"The bluebottles, which bluebottles?"

"Oh, there were hundreds of them in the laundry room and there was a terrible smell coming from in there too, but I have no idea what it was. It had gone on for days and was there when Anthony came home on Friday but over the weekend they all disappeared. The smell and the bluebottles were suddenly gone. Neither Anthony nor myself can get into that room and neither of us knew what to make of it. It was a mystery to him as well."

"Didn't you tell me that the professor had the only key to that place?" Fleming asked.

"Yes, he is the only one with a key and he is in America apparently. The archaeologist has gone back to Sutherland, by the way. She didn't stay too long, despite the fact that Anthony is unaccounted for."

Detective Superintendent Barrowman was gaining little ground in his missing person, or possible murder, enquiry. John Wetherby had been calling for him but then so had everyone else. He would get back to them after he checked out a possible lead.

All available schoolboys from Letherford School had been interviewed and particulars noted of their parents whereabouts and vehicle ownership. A great number of boys were already abroad in the company of their parents but of those so far interviewed only one had anything to offer.

The boy was a pupil finishing first form and knew William J. Faraday.

The child witness had been collected from the school by his father and as they were leaving the school grounds the boy had seen William Faraday walking alone on the left footpath, a short distance from the school entrance. A silver coloured car had drawn up alongside William but the witness's father had simply overtaken the stationary silver vehicle and kept going. This had not allowed the witness time to see if William had entered that car or not. The boy could not describe the driver beyond stating that he was a man on his own and he had not even looked at the car registration.

Barrowman was not aware of any sightings of William

Faraday beyond the point described by this witness and local CCTV footage had failed to show the boy in any shop. Local street footage already scanned for a boy pedestrian in school uniform would now be scanned a second time for any silver vehicle carrying a male driver and boy passenger. Some of the large villas on the right side of the street, as one leaves Letherford School, may have their own CCTV and police officers were directed to enquire if any active cameras had faced the street from these driveways. If so, they would be checked.

Like his mother, Anthony Halbooth had never been a person who bought a newspaper but he had bought one now and he had it spread across the table in the coffee shop where he had just paid a ridiculous price for a cup of coffee. The paper gave a full account of the missing schoolboy and included shorter accounts of the previous abductions, highlighting the similarities between the present case and those of the past two years. Anthony learned what others already knew about the children being abducted on the last day of the school year, that year being the senior first form. Anthony wondered about the significance of the girl pupil, Helen Holloway. Why would the killer go for a girl from the Mary Upton School for Girls? It was miles away.

He had never actually admitted to himself that he had suspicions about his own father, just a nagging mental

THE TALE OF THE OLD SCHOOL TIES

irritation, beginning with the professor's mysterious nocturnal visit to dispose of something that attracted bluebottles. He knew about his father's tantrum-like anger over rejection. Rejections like the one his father had received from the very school that had now lost another pupil. These were the reasons that had brought Anthony here. The unhappy historical connection with Letherford School was significant to Anthony's unease, but there was no reason that he knew of for the Mary Upton School for Girls to become a target for his father. Why would any kidnapper of young boys be going there?

He felt a bit relieved as he folded up the newspaper and just a tiny bit guilty. He had seriously considered his own father as a possible suspect for taking the boy Faraday. Anthony felt some excitement from this affair and excitement was not normally part of his mental diet.

The case of William Faraday was intriguing and Anthony's time and money were his own to spend. He drained the last froth from his coffee cup. Someone would know where this girls' school was.

While Anthony wondered where he was going, Fleming was wondering where Anthony was. Fleming was not actually worried for the boy's safety, just seriously interested in why he had chosen to leave home for no apparent reason. Chief Inspector MacKellar had been on Fleming's back a little more than normal over the missing boy, of course, to people like MacKellar these missing persons were outstanding statistics, an inconvenience in life's smooth flow. Fleming thought of Anthony more like a missing bank card, one should take the necessary action and stop worrying. Bank cards? Passbooks? Gretchen had mentioned that Anthony had an account of his own at the building society branch beside the woollen shop. Fleming was also a customer there and he knew the pleasant young lady who worked there.

He took his photographs along to the branch office and told the young lady that Anthony was missing from home. Had she seen him since last Friday? Was he making withdrawals elsewhere?

"I will ask the manager to call about that," the girl promised. "Last Friday? I'm pretty sure he was in here and made a withdrawal." She wrote the figure '£100' on a scrap of paper and showed it to Fleming before turning it into a shredder.

"Thanks Katie. It will still help to know where he has gone. Let us know when you can."

Fleming went directly to the railway station and the ticket clerk.

"Last Friday, did you sell a ticket to this boy?"

"Yes, he took the teatime train to Glasgow."

"Just to Glasgow?" Fleming asked the older man.

"Yes, but he first asked me about a ticket price to London. It seemed a bit much. I think he was going for the overnight London bus."

"Thank you."

THE TALE OF THE OLD SCHOOL TIES

Alan Forbes was a local fisherman who set out creels in quiet edges of the bay during the early hours of the morning and lifted them in the late afternoon. He had retired from ferry service and his fishing was more of a hobby than an occupation. He was thinking that it was just as well, for the recent calm weather had been providing him with few shellfish. Creel after creel was light and he knew by the feel of each one that it would be empty, then there was this one.

Alan pulled harder and even considered his windlass but chose to persevere by hand. When the creel broke the surface Alan could see that it had become entangled with some wire mesh which in turn was covered in seaweed. The mesh was formed into a tubular parcel that contained a lump of concrete. When he got the whole affair onto the deck Alan pulled off the seaweed and could see that the concrete was not alone in the wire mesh. There was a small skeleton inside. There were no limbs or head, just the skeleton of a small torso.

At any other time he, like Archie Campbell, would have assumed that someone had parted company with a pet dog, but in view of recent press reports he chose not to throw this unwelcome find back into the sea. He carefully disentangled the empty creel and re-baited it. When his creel run was over he called up the Coastguards and asked them to contact the police and ask that they meet him at the jetty.

The large stone building was impressive with tall casement windows and a solid wooden front door above which a round window displayed the school crest in stained glass. The door was closed and locked. There were no vehicles in sight. Anthony felt disappointed but decided to walk around the school.

Behind the building there was a car parked and from the garden beyond the car came the sound of whistling. Anthony ventured through a gap in the hedge and found an elderly man weeding between parallel rows of vegetables. After watching him for a few moments Anthony felt comfortable about approaching this man. The gardener became aware of him and stopped whistling as he looked up.

"Well, young man, what brings you here?"

"A bit of a project really," Anthony said with a smile. "I attend a boys' school and I wanted to know how a girls' school came to be. I had hoped that the headmaster or some of the staff would still be here. Do all the boarders go home?" he asked as if he had expected to find pupils too.

"Maybe not," the man replied, "but the boarding house is not here. It's in the village, an old grey three storey house with a grey and pink flag flying above it. Any boarders would be there, I suppose. There won't be any staff though."

"Are these the school colours, pink and grey?"

"Yes, always have been."

"Have you worked here long?" Anthony asked.

The man laughed at the question and the notion that he was the only person for the boy to enquire with.

"Yes, I've been here for years, lad. I am the school caretaker and I am not on holiday, least not yet."

"Does the school employ other men on the staff? Is it not all women?"

"On the teaching side it is mostly women, as you say, but there have been men teaching here." the man said, wondering about the boy's questions, but then remembered that he had mentioned the word 'project'. "I suppose you think it would have to be women to teach in a girls' school but folks nowadays would say that that was discriminating against the male teachers. Your own school will have lady teachers I'll bet."

"Yes, it does but they are older ladies." Anthony answered as if that made less of a distinction.

"So this school would be all right if it had old men, eh?" the caretaker laughed.

"Have there been problems caused by employing younger men as teachers here?" Anthony asked, expecting a negative answer.

"There was a problem once, about ten years back," the old man remembered, "When a young man got the heave because of complaints about him."

"What was there to complain about?" Anthony asked, sounding surprised.

"Well, he was molesting the girls, at least that is what

they claimed. He got told to leave immediately. He was a science teacher, seemed a quiet chap but you can never tell, I suppose."

"Can you remember his name?" Anthony asked, making the caretaker frown.

"His first name was Harvey, that's all I remember. Why would you want to know that for your project?"

"It's all right. My science teacher is not called Harvey." Harvey said with a smile.

The caretaker laughed.

"I think that man gave up teaching after that. Anyway he moved away after his wife .." at that he broke off as if unwilling to continue.

"After his wife did what? Did she leave him?"

"She left all of us, my boy, she committed suicide. The shame of it, folks supposed at the time, who knows?"

"Is this school connected in any way to Letherford School for Boys?" Anthony asked as if purposefully changing the subject. "I know they have both had pupils go missing but the schools themselves, are they in any way connected?"

The caretaker shook his head.

"There is no connection as I know of. Like you say, there's the missing kids, but nothing other than that. The children weren't connected in any way either. I remember them saying that in the paper."

"Who was Mary Upton?" Anthony asked, aware that he had visited his personal interest topics often enough.

"She was the founder, a lady with money and influence. They say she was one of them suffragettes. You heard of them?"

"Yes. They protested for the emancipation of women." Anthony said with pride.

"Well she reckoned to teach women separate from men. She is dead long ago like, but she would be right pleased with this place now."

"She would be pleased with your garden too. It looks very well kept." Anthony commented.

"This is the time I like, when they are all away home and I get peace to work in here. The girls planted some these things, mind you, third form girls."

"I just finished third year. We don't have a garden to grow things but it would be really cool to have one. I better go and let you get on but you have been a great help."

"Happy to help. It has been a pleasure meeting you too."

As Anthony walked away he heard the whistling resume.

Douglas Campbell and Darren Black attended at the pier as Alan Forbes brought in his small creel boat. Before anyone touched the wire mesh Alan pointed out just how much seaweed he had removed from it.

"This thing has travelled quite a bit since it went into the water. My creels are sitting on sand and rock with no weed beside them. The current has dragged this thing around through weed banks before letting it slip into slack water."

"So where did it go into the water, most likely?" Campbell asked. "Where is the weed?"

"The weed banks mostly skirt behind the rocks and it would need the strength of a good current to pull this through them. My guess is that it was thrown into an ebb tide from a boat or a bridge somewhere to the east of my creels."

Campbell nodded his understanding.

"Do you think this could be another bairn?" Forbes asked anxiously.

"It looks about the right size and shape." Darren Black told him. "The pathologist will tell us for sure."

"Can we take just that wire parcel, Alan, just as it is? I have spread out some polythene in the boot of the car."

Andrew Fleming had gone out to the Halbooth home. There was a telephone there and he wanted to know from Gretchen if Anthony had been in touch.

Gretchen was still concerned about the boy and she had not heard from him or either of his parents. She promised to inform Fleming of any contact.

On his way back into town Fleming looked in at the library. There was no real reason to expect that Anthony had contacted Mrs Campbell but he may have said something before leaving. Fleming had noticed how Mrs

Campbell's quiet nature had given Anthony the confidence to speak to her freely.

"I think he is all right," the librarian said softly, handing Fleming a postcard addressed to 'Officer 159 c/o Public Library, Corran Bay'. Fleming smiled.

"I told you he looked at your shoulder number," she said quietly and with a smile. "Anthony has his wits about him. He will be safe enough."

Fleming was looking at the message part of the card. It read, 'disiecta membra – aspirat primo Fortuna labori'.

"I see from the post mark that he is in London, Mrs Campbell. I hope he really does have his wits about him."

"On his return to the police office, Fleming met the CID officers as they emptied the wire mesh cage from the boot of their car. As Fleming helped to clean out the wet polythene they explained how Alan Forbes had found the small skeleton.

"No head yet," Fleming commented. "But it will turn up somewhere with a mouthful of teeth and then we might be getting somewhere."

"Talking of missing heads," Campbell said sarcastically, "have you not found your missing student yet?"

"Unlike this poor wee soul," Fleming said, pointing to the wire mesh. "Anthony will find his own way home."

Later that evening when schoolteachers might well be at home Fleming called.

"Mr Henderson? Andrew Fleming here, I'm afraid. I have another phrase for you to decipher."

Fleming read the postcard.

"Scattered limbs – fortune has smiled on our first efforts. That's what I make of it."

"Thank you Mr Henderson."

FOUR

Anthony Halbooth was conscious of his dwindling finances but was determined to make the best use of his opportunity. From the Mary Upton School he went to the local town library and enquired about old newspapers. He was directed to the office of a news editor who compiled the local paper. The printing was now done centrally for several diverse papers to keep costs down.

The news editor listened patiently to Anthony's account of conducting research for a journalistic project to be completed over the summer recess.

"So you want to read, if possible then to buy, the copy coverage of the two stories, last year's missing schoolgirl and the report on a disgraced teacher at the same school ten years ago, is that correct?" the editor asked. "Are you suggesting a connection there?"

"I don't think so." Anthony replied innocently. "They are simply the events that people remember in relation to this particular independent school. I am conducting similar enquiries elsewhere." Anthony said casually as if what he was pursuing was simply a reflection of public interest.

"So public domain information will suffice?" the editor asked as he rose from his chair. He locked the door of the room and beckoned Anthony towards a door leading out from the back of his office to a storeroom.

In the storeroom there were rows of shelves supporting countless files of old newspaper copies, catalogued sequentially. The editor pulled down a folder marked 'July 1981'.

"This takes care of last year's missing girl but then the other business was ten years ago, but when?" his eyes ran along the shelves for inspiration but he ended up looking down at the floor, deep in thought. "I seem to remember that there was some major event that kept that teacher's story off the front page. Now was that the Trident crash?"

He moved to another aisle and looked up the shelves for part of the nineteen seventies.

"June 72, I'm sure it was." he said as if trying to convince himself. He pulled down the folder for June 1972 and looked at the front page of each old copy.

"Our paper is weekly, Anthony, it comes out on Thursdays," he explained, "Here we are. The plane crash was on the Sunday night, 18th June. Now what else is here?"

He flicked over the pages and ran his forefinger down each column.

"Here we are, Anthony, 'Teacher accused. Bertram Harvey Johns, 28 years old chemistry and biology teacher at the Mary Upton School for Girls has been dismissed following allegations of sexual misconduct towards pupils in the fifth and sixth form of the school'. There are only three paragraphs on the matter, I'm afraid. The Staines air crash has squeezed the coverage, I guess."

"Can I purchase a copy?" Anthony asked.

"No, I am sorry but these are single records back then. Even the more recent ones would take a week or two to get for you. I do not mind giving you a photocopy of this small article though."

"Thank you. Mr Johns' wife died shortly after this story came to light. Can we look forward in the month and see if her death was mentioned?" Anthony asked.

"Why do you want to see that?"

"Just to confirm what I have been told." Anthony said plainly.

"Good journalistic practice," the editor remarked and began to turn pages. "There it is, Cynthia Johns, died suddenly at home on Saturday 24th June 1972."

"It doesn't say it was suicide?" Anthony questioned.

"No, we don't make an issue of such deaths, but you are right, it was suicide as I remember."

"How was it, or how did she.."

Anthony felt awkward about asking.

"She hung herself from the stair bannister," the editor said as if he had no wish to say more. "Let's see what coverage we gave the schoolgirl."

The pair returned to the folder from the previous July and found the story on the first three pages of the first week's copy.

"Oh dear," said Anthony, looking disappointed.

"Just a moment." the editor said sympathetically as he walked to some shelves at the back where Anthony could not see him. He returned with a newspaper in his hand. "You are in luck, Anthony. We made an extra run on that one. You can have this and we can copy the 'teacher story' now, okay?"

Morton Grant was at the top of a ladder, painting a lamp-post in a quiet street on the outskirts of Corran Bay. He could see into the rooms of the nearest houses although he made no obvious signs of looking. The house directly ahead of him was the upper flat in a block of four. With the midday sun behind Morton, the front room of the flat was illuminated by sunshine while the presence of Morton himself would have been a difficult sight for anyone looking out from the room into the bright glare.

There was someone in the room. A man in a short sleeved shirt was holding a series of white cylindrical hoops while closely studying the surface of each one. Morton could see that the man wore surgical gloves while doing this. Finally the fellow placed the white objects into a black plastic bag before wrapping it up and sealing it with tape. The man took the parcel out of the room and a moment later, he appeared outside at his dustbin. He would have deposited the parcel into the bin but he noticed Morton at the top of the lamp-post and changed his mind. He took the parcel back into the house but did not re-appear in the front room. Morton finished painting but noted the number of the post as he climbed down. He walked along the street and made a pretence of picking something up from the road surface while he looked into the driveway beside the house and noted the number of the silver car that was parked there. He returned to the ladder and took a notebook from his overall pocket. This was normally used to log his work but for now, it was to take note of the lamp-post number and the registration number of the car.

John Wetherby had reported to the Board of Trustees on every aspect of the disappearance of William J. Faraday. His reports had been read and discussed without any personal blame being attached to the headmaster. The Chairman of the Board, Lord Brackston, had called at the school to inform Wetherby to that effect personally and to commend him for remaining on station while police, parental and press interest was at its height.

"I thought we had seen the last of this barbarity two years ago, Wetherby. It seems not. Some imbecile is still on the loose and sees Letherford as a target. Has there been any progress made since your report?"

"No sir, I am afraid not. The police have told me confidentially that they have an interest in a silver car but without details they have little or no confidence in tracing it. Their interest now places the abduction closer to the school grounds, for what that is worth, but they admit to having a mountain to climb to find the guilty party." Wetherby sounded annoyed and pessimistic.

"Any suggestions come to you from staff or former staff?" Lord Brackston asked, his question delivered in a judicial manner.

"Not really." Wetherby answered. "I actually found that of possible significance, to be quite honest, the fact that there have been no suggestions along these lines. I had a visit from a young man, a fifteen year old schoolboy from a different school entirely, asking about his father's application for a position here ten years ago. He had no interest in the current situation but it made me think of possible motives arising from past connections, fathers, brothers and so on."

"Some sort of retrospective motive you mean?" Lord Brackston said, looking at Wetherby seriously. "Does that present any possibilities that you know of?"

"I have been here for six years, as you know and I cannot think of anyone with such a heavy grievance in that time." Wetherby replied.

"The passage of time would normally weaken the incentive and resolve for any serious act of revenge." Lord Brackston said firmly, as if he really meant 'take my word for it'. Wetherby chose not to dispute the point.

"This is the third consecutive abduction of its type," Wetherby said, "and the apparent seizure and murder of 12 year old children takes a particular kind of individual, would you agree, my lord?"

"Yes I would. I see what you are getting at, Wetherby. Not only someone with a grievance but someone capable of atrocity and the sort of characteristics that ought to be narrowing the field, would you say?"

"That is what I mean. I cannot believe that a rational human being, even one who is seeking revenge, would take this course of action if he felt as repulsed by it as the rest of us."

"Chances are that he has done this sort of thing before." the Chairman agreed. "Before he came near any independent schools, I mean. Good thinking, Wetherby. I'll have a word with this chap Barrowman."

Anthony Halbooth boarded the bus for his return journey to Glasgow knowing that the purchase of his bus ticket meant that he now had only £2.83 in his possession plus the return rail ticket from Glasgow to Corran Bay. He placed his rucksack against the window wall and leaned on it. He was tired and expected to sleep. This bus was busier than the one he had travelled south on. Memories of the long journey south made him even more exhausted. He soon fell asleep.

Later that day, as a drained and exhausted Anthony Halbooth transferred from the bus to a northbound train, Lord Brackston had his conversation with Detective Superintendent James Barrowman.

"Don't you agree Superintendent that anyone who

could snatch children from school and murder them to dispose of their bodies a piece at a time has to have some sort of indicative history?"

"Yes, of course, Lord Brackston, but what form would that history take? I expect that the culprit here has something in his past to demonstrate his callous indifference to life, but the field is not narrowed by it. I cannot hope to find this man by entering his crimes into a database. We do not know the full extent of his crimes against these children. None of the children have turned up in any identifiable way. We have no physical evidence to say how they were murdered or why they were abducted. Were they taken for reasons of abuse? We do not know. When we look at the pattern the constants are; the age of the child; their attendance at an independent school; their stage of learning within that school and their disappearance on the same day in terms of the school year." the police officer reminded Lord Brackston.

"Surely someone can elucidate the type of character we are looking for, based on the little that we do know?" Lord Brackston blurted pathetically.

Barrowman looked and felt frustrated but he knew he would have to give his visitor some satisfaction for his visit.

"The sort of thing you are suggesting is not used seriously here in England. It is called profiling, sir. The FBI in America has professional people in that role and they can make use of their support, but the skill is not yet recognised here, not in a reliable way."

"What about the press?" Lord Brackston said. "Could they not use it, if only to raise a few hares?"

Barrowman looked at Lord Brackston with his 'you're not going away are you?' look.

"The only way that would be feasible would be in the form of an article, a magazine article, covering the nature of people who might do this sort of thing. If the press were happy to print such an article by some amateur profiler I would not provide any information beyond what already lies in the public domain. I would not be obliged by yourself or them to act on their conclusions and I could certainly would not suffer any harassment arising out of it from journalists. It might help the investigation or it may well damage it by giving the public the impression that they should focus on particular type of person. That could well cause them to ignore genuine suspects. If it all went horribly wrong then everyone involved, with respect, even yourself, would simply wash their hands of it and hide."

Raymond Adam read the pathologists report carefully. The small skeleton held in the wire mesh was indeed human. The pathologist was satisfied that the bones belonged to the torso of a twelve year old girl, give or take a year. 'How does he know that?' Adam wondered. The forensic pathologist had also formed the opinion that the bones had been subjected to salt water for months, perhaps as long as a year. This seemed to be consistent with the missing girl from Surrey. He looked sideways at a list of names and numbers for Surrey and Kent police CID involved, but decided against making any call until the lab result came to him. The lab had the wire mesh, seaweed and concrete. There was no point in simply prompting questions from his English colleagues until he had all possible information.

Lord Brackston wasted no time in arranging an appointment with a social friend of longstanding who happened to be the editor of a national newspaper.

"I would like a fairly comprehensive résumé of this case with a character profile of the person responsible. According to Barrowman the Americans can do this but we must have some expert in the field who can describe this man in the way that your readers can identify him. Damn it, Jeremy, this killer is capable of bringing the old school down. The fear element is hardly marketable."

The editor had listened patiently and sensed an opportunity to get a word in.

"Lord Brackston, from a newspaper perspective what you are suggesting is the equivalent of shooting blindly from the hip. We cannot publish any true account of these terrible crimes beyond what we have done already. If we go off on some tangent then the police will desert us and we will find it difficult to keep pace with enquiries. We may well lose ground to our competitors. This profiling business, I think that is what the Americans call it, is not something that readers could know well enough to have faith in. I do not know who can or would attempt the undertaking of creating a profile. Your killer is horrific enough judging by his actions. No, the nearest I can come for you is to have an article written on the typical behaviour of serial killers. There have been several of these types and I know who can do that particular job for me; but, and I mean this, there can be no allusion to your culprit, the profiling, so to speak would only be of typical cases based on historical and known killers."

Lord Brackston looked deflated but he could appreciate most of the legal pitfalls his friend was anticipating.

"There is nothing to prevent you from running a current news item on the cases on one page and your 'softly, softly' profile article on another.

"Innuendo. It is not uncommon." Jeffrey said, sounding agreeable but not enthusiastic. "Very well."

Anthony Halbooth had walked wearily home that evening and went straight to bed. He slept until 5 a.m. He then lay awake, considering his trip to London, Kent and Surrey and the information he had gleaned. The main purpose of his visit had been to determine the tormenting question of his father's connection, if any, with these terrible murders of abducted children. According to his father's secretary, the man had been in America for weeks, his only return being on the date that Anthony had seen him at the laundry room. That did not seem to allow the necessary additional time for his father to have abducted the boy from Letherford and dispose of the body in parcels. On the matter of missing children, it had intrigued him that they should have occurred on the last day of term, the end of the first form year for the victim, a pupil of an independent school, yet they had nothing else in common.

Now that he was at home and no longer hot on the trail of a kidnapper, the story of the dismissed science teacher seemed less exciting, less relevant, a rush of blood, a bit like his suspicions of his father. How could he be sure that to his imaginative mind, this was not just a red herring? There might well be similar stories, hundreds of them, leading to similar inappropriate judgements, as yet unknown to Anthony. He had spoken briefly to a gardener and used that conversation to expand his theory around the teacher with the news editor serving the local paper in that Surrey area. He lay in silent debate for an hour and a half addressing himself subjectively and objectively, before rising to make breakfast. It was Friday 16th July. Gretchen would arrive at 8 o'clock.

When Gretchen MacIntyre arrived and found the house door unlocked she entered with a look of apprehension on her face. This changed to shock and delight as she found Anthony sitting at the kitchen table with a broad smile on his face.

"Oh Anthony, you are back. I was so worried about you. Where did you go?"

"I went to London, Gretchen. I'm sorry that I never left you a note or something. It was a fairly sudden decision on my part but I should have realised that you would worry."

"Oh Anthony, I reported you missing. I better tell the police that you are home." She lifted the telephone and dialled the local police number. "And your mother was here for a day or two but she has gone back. Oh, police station? Yes, this is Gretchen MacIntyre at the lodge, will you tell Constable Fleming that Anthony is home safe and well?"

Mrs Valetta Vivien Johns finished reading the article in the newspaper with a sinking, nauseating feeling. She stared at her patio doors, leading into the garden of her Hampshire home and cursed them for admitting sufficient light to have allowed her to read such an article. The entry in the newspaper had attempted to demonstrate the typical child behaviour of those who had later proved to be serial killers or rapists with particularly sadistic methods.

She heard her housekeeper, Mary Ainsworth, entering by the front door and threw the newspaper aside just as Mary stuck her head round the room door to say, "Good morning, Mrs Johns, are you well?"

"Yes, Mary, I am quite well, thank you." Mrs Johns replied.

It was a routine exchange conducted every morning.

The next part of the routine would involve Mary bringing through a mug of tea for each of them.

Valetta Johns lifted her tambour from the top of her sewing box and began to sew in another pansy petal in two shades of blue. Minutes later Mary brought their tea.

"It's so dark in this room on such a lovely morning." Mary remarked. "Have you ever given a thought to changing the wallpaper in this room to something lighter?"

"This dark stuff may not reflect the weather, Mary, but it does give a fair reflection of my life thus far." Mrs Johns answered. Mary was silent, unsure of the mood. "I suppose you have a point, Mary," Mrs Johns continued. "Perhaps when we have finished our tea you can give me a hand to take this embroidery out to the patio table. I don't think there is any wind today and the sun will be pleasant."

"Now you are talking," Mary said with a smile.

Mrs Johns smiled back. The last thing she would want to do was to offend Mary, the woman had been a Godsend. Although Valetta Johns was a mere 62 years of age, she had suffered bouts of depression, alcoholism and arthritis during the last ten years. Her husband, Wesley, had been 25 years her senior when they had married. She had been 20 and he 45 years of age when their marriage had been predicted, prompted, advised, proposed and decided by everyone else but Valetta. She had been squeezed into a corner by family pressure and their arrogant, uncaring society friends. She had married and

THE TALE OF THE OLD SCHOOL TIES

then lived with the situation, yielding sufficiently to provide a male heir for her husband. The son had grown and graduated but while still a young man had brought disgrace to his parents.

The class-conscious circle of 'friends' that had continued as the baggage of their union, had soon drifted away after the death of the old brigadier. Her husband had simply succumbed to age, alcohol and shame. He had died five years ago. After his death Valetta had fought back against her problems with drink and depression. Hiring Mary had been a positive step in that process and now Valetta had only one problem, arthritis, and one friend, Mary Ainsworth.

Mary carried the tambour and sewing box out to the patio, keeping pace with Mrs Johns and her walking stick.

"I'll leave you to your stitching, dear," Mary said, "and I'll get started with my own work. Have you any particular preference for lunch today?"

"Now, Mary, you know you don't have to .." she began but was not allowed to finish.

"Greek salad, all right?" Mary said as she disappeared back through the French doors. She was already gone when Mrs Johns replied, "Yes, all right."

Mary picked up the newspaper she had seen Mrs Johns throw away so hastily. The manner of her doing this, together with her dark comment on her wallpaper reflecting life, were both out of character for Valetta Johns nowadays. A few years back they would not have been and Mary had no wish to see the clock turned back. In the kitchen Mary looked through the pages for anything that could have sparked the drop in the older woman's mood.

There was nothing of local interest, nothing of a personal nature, the obituary column had no familiar names and Valetta never looked at the television and sport anyway. Had it been the stock market? No idea. There was an article on the child behaviour of people who had gone on to become psychopathic killers in later life but it did not concern any particular person. The article was interesting though and Mary kept reading. Terms like 'sociopath' and 'phenotypically' meant nothing to Mary but the idea of young children sadistically mutilating young animals and birds, made her shiver. Wilful attacks on property, serious violation of home rules and school discipline, defiance of authority and elders, violence born of resentment, all for the gratification of sensation, were apparently indications of the child development of a psychopath. The article had concluded with advice to parents of such children to make the social services aware of the behaviour. Counselling and if appropriate, treatment, would be provided.

Mary folded the newspaper and returned it to the lamp table beside Valetta's chair.

Shortly before ten o'clock Andrew Fleming arrived at the lodge house to find Gretchen and Anthony sitting at the kitchen table.

"It's good to see you back, Anthony. Gretchen was quite worried about you." Fleming said with a smile. "I had the feeling that you were all right and your postcard was reassuring, thank you."

Gretchen drew Fleming a puzzled look. She knew nothing of any postcard. She had certainly not received one.

"I basically went to find out when my father might be coming home." Anthony said, his tone suggesting that his going should not have worried anyone. "But I should have left a note for Gretchen. I see that now."

"Right Anthony," said Fleming, his notebook poised. "In general terms, you left Corran Bay last Friday on the late afternoon train to Glasgow and then took the overnight bus to London. You had £100 from your building society account to sustain you. What happened after that?"

Anthony stared back, open-mouthed.

"You knew about me drawing money?"

"When someone goes missing without leaving a note, Anthony, there are unanswered questions as to their intentions. A missing person with suicide in mind does not normally draw money. You can't take it with you, right? Whereas someone who intends to survive while missing, or has been kidnapped for their money, will require funding. That is the best we can do without a note. A note is always best." he explained with a wave of his pencil.

"I went to London, to my father's office and spoke to

his secretary about where he was. He has been in America for the past three or four weeks and ought to be back again next week. He flew back for a speaking engagement on Saturday 3rd July but flew straight back to the States." Anthony stopped as if he had completed his explanation. Fleming was looking at him.

"You were gone for six days, Anthony. What else did you get up to?"

Anthony looked briefly at Gretchen, suggesting to Fleming that Anthony would prefer her to be absent but Gretchen never reacted. Fleming was remembering the Latin text on the postcard.

"Did you visit the places you have never been to before?" Fleming asked in a relaxed manner.

"Yes, I did," Anthony replied, grateful not to be lying.

"And from London back to Corran Bay was simply a direct reversal of the journey down? You got home late?"

"Yes, that's right," Anthony agreed enthusiastically, happy not to be pressed.

"That will be sufficient for my report," Fleming said, tucking his notebook into his pocket.

Gretchen smiled in satisfaction and relief. She had been the one to report Anthony missing and the blame for any harm befalling him would have attached itself unfairly to her, at least in the eyes of the eccentric parents. It appeared that such fears were now irrelevant and she rose to resume her household duties.

Fleming was far from finished and, with a beckoning

nod of his head, told Anthony to join to join him in the small dining room

"Now Anthony you can tell me how fortune smiled on your first efforts."

Anthony looked a little diffident, the result of his early morning self-appraisal of what he knew. Fleming saw the reluctance.

"A scholar can only be judged on what he writes, Anthony. Tell me all of it."

This was enough to prompt the boy and he began to relate a chronological account of what had been done and said by everyone during his visits to Letherford School in Kent and the Mary Upton School in Surrey. Fleming had taken his notebook out again and was writing furiously as Anthony spoke. Names and dates were confirmed as they arose but otherwise Fleming left the boy to recite his version.

"You have submitted a first-class paper, Anthony." Fleming said with a smile.

"Oh, papers, I almost forgot. I brought newspapers and copies of articles with me from Surrey. I'll get them." with that Anthony dashed off upstairs to fetch the papers he was talking about. Fleming looked around the room and his eye again fell on the family group photograph taken years ago in front of a Morris 1000 traveller. Fleming could tell from the vehicle registration that it was a 1966 model. Anthony arrived back with his newspaper and photocopies.

"Here are the old papers I got. They tell the stories of Richard Barton and Helen Holloway. These others are the photocopies of entries pertaining to the schoolteacher accused of molesting girls at the Mary Upton School. He was dismissed. There is a copy of the entry showing that his wife died on the last day of term that year. She committed suicide but the paper doesn't say that as a matter of policy."

"But you do know?" Fleming asked.

"The caretaker had told me that and the news editor confirmed it later. Everybody who needed to know would know that she had hung herself from the staircase bannister in their home, the newspaper had no wish to print it."

"I could certainly use a copy of these." Fleming hinted.

"We could copy them at the library." Anthony suggested with boyish enthusiasm.

There was a perfectly good photocopier at the police station but Fleming knew how much Anthony Halbooth liked to live in his own world and his own terms.

"All right, Anthony. I will pay Mrs Campbell this time and I will run you there and back. I dare say you will be needing to place your order for more classic books."

"That would be splendid." Anthony replied.

"This time, tell Gretchen where you are going."

An hour later and Anthony was delivered back to the lodge house. The papers had been copied for Fleming and Mrs Campbell had been delighted to see that her faith in Anthony had been quite justified.

THE TALE OF THE OLD SCHOOL TIES

Fleming would keep the papers to himself and read them at his leisure. He walked up the street to assist with the arrival of a large lorry, delivering to the store by way of a tight turn through a narrow lane. He had helped this driver regularly and still did not know how the man managed to do as well as he did.

Fleming was aware that Morton Grant was walking towards him but it was still early in the day. Morton would be sober and his normal practice when sober was to lower his head and walk past without speaking to, or even acknowledging Fleming. This time was slightly different.

Morton did not stop walking but he did look and, as he passed, he held out a small white envelope. It had nothing written on it and was sealed. Fleming looked backwards to Morton but the painter was still walking away. He wouldn't be looking back, he never did. Fleming tore open the envelope and found a small note inside, written in pencil was, 'black parcel man 24 Heather Road'. Fleming laughed to himself, a tip from the mafia, whatever next?

As he awaited the arrival of the lorry, Fleming thought about the sober Morton Grant, council painter, who had just handed him this note. He would need to speak to Morton alone at some time to learn the substance behind this note. Morton Grant was not the kidding type when sober.

When Fleming reported for duty the following morning he was shocked to find that the nightshift were still on duty, dealing with the discovery of an adult male body on the railway line beneath a bridge just out of town. The body was that of Morton Grant. The driver of an incoming goods train had seen the body around 4.00 a.m., lying on the broken stone beside the track. Morton had sustained extensive head injuries and now lay in the hospital mortuary.

The whole town knew Morton Grant and, despite his strange manner, everybody generally liked him, so there was little reason for anyone to suspect foul play. Fleming would not expect foul play either had he not received an unexplained note from Morton the previous day. There would be no opportunity now to discuss the matter with the man. Accidental death? Fleming was not so sure.

It was Saturday morning and Fleming did not expect to see Douglas Campbell or Darren Black today. He checked the voters' roll for 24 Heather Road. The house was occupied by Bert Jones, a name that meant nothing to Fleming. Then again, these were small flats in Heather Road and the occupants tended to change more regularly than other streets. Would it still be occupied by Bert Jones?

Fleming took Hamish MacLeod with him to Heather Road to acquaint himself with number 24. It was not yet eight o'clock in the morning and there were few signs of life in Heather Road. Parked in the driveway beside 22 and 24 was a silver Ford estate car. The ground elsewhere was dry but around this car there was a ring of dampness, suggesting that the vehicle had been washed recently, very recently. Fleming noted the registration number. No. 24 was an upstairs flat and in the flat itself the curtains were still drawn. Without making any noise or asking Hamish to join him, Fleming went to the car and looked into the back. There was nothing there. The back seats were folded down and the floor carpet was missing. On the washing line behind the building, a car carpet was hanging in the breeze. Fleming lifted the lid of the dustbin and found five or six black plastic bags of rubbish, each tied at the neck with string. Had this been what Morton had seen? Fleming re-joined Hamish and returned to the office. The car registration showed on the Police National Computer to be registered to Bert Jones of 24 Heather Road.

Morton Grant normally drank in the Ladder Bar, a small pub frequented mostly by young fishermen who would readily listen to Morton's extravagant tales, full of imaginative events. Fleming went there shortly after 11 a.m. when he hoped the barman from the previous night would be back on duty. He was.

"You heard about Morton?" he asked the barman, showing sympathy. The man nodded.

"Aye, he was in here just last night, the poor bugger."

"Was he drunk, I mean really drunk?" Fleming asked.

The barman shook his head.

"He never is, you know that yourself. He has either five or six pints and that's him, last night it was six, no problem to the big man."

"Did he fall out with anyone?" Fleming asked.

"Not in here," the barman said positively. "He was actually in good form last night, telling the guys that he had mafia business to attend to, 'a big contract job' to see to. He is some man, well he was some man."

"Did he leave at his usual time?"

"Right on the stroke of eleven." the barman replied.

"Alone?"

"As always." the barman confirmed.

The road across the railway at the point where Morton was presumed to have fallen was a quiet country road leading to farms. It was not part of Morton's route home nor was it close to Heather Road. Fleming had wondered if Morton's 'big mafia job' had involved Heather Road.

With Hamish for company again, Fleming drove down the road crossing the railway and stopped near to the bridge. The two officers were sure that their colleagues on the nightshift would have visited this part of the road at the time but Fleming had to see for himself. In the bright sunshine it was ideal for thoroughly searching the road surface and parapets. The only thing they discovered on the road was a small black plastic split peg, of the type used to keep a carpet in place on the floor of a car.

"Probably nothing," Fleming told Hamish. "But I'll keep it anyway."

They drove ahead over the bridge and turned the police car around at the first opportunity. As they did so the tyres splashed through a puddle of farm muck dropped from a spreader.

"That's made a fine mess of the car." Hamish said with a chuckle.

"Yes, maybe we are not the first to fall victim to that puddle." Fleming commented, recalling the car in the Heather Road driveway, apparently washed prior to 8 a.m.

Dougie Campbell was not on duty but Detective Chief Inspector Raymond Adam was and Fleming called him. He explained to Adam the circumstances of the previous twenty-four hours and the DCI promised to be there in Corran Bay, as soon as he could. He would call MacKellar and Campbell himself.

The nightshift officers were called out early in order to advise Adam and Campbell on the circumstances they had dealt with the previous night. The Procurator Fiscal was informed by Douglas Campbell of the enquiry and the possibility of a homicide. The Procurator Fiscal asked to be kept informed of any progress being made and the need, should it arise, for any warrants in connection with the enquiry.

Dougie Campbell told Raymond Adam how unreliable and imaginative Morton Grant had been in the past and how, in his opinion, a slip of paper from such an individual was not a firm basis to go knocking on the door of Bert Jones. The DCI was influenced by what he had been told but still liked what Fleming had said about the washed car and the use of black bags for all household waste. If such a bag was used to dispose of a body part it would appear no different from any other rubbish from Jones' house.

"Your evidence is circumstantial and easily fobbed off if our Mr Jones is an inveterate liar, Andy. We do not even know him, do you?" Campbell told Fleming, obviously annoyed at being disturbed from his time off.

"No and neither did Morton Grant." Fleming replied.

"We need the post mortem result here to tell us if we have a murder, do we not?" the DCI reminded Campbell.

"That's what the Fiscal said." Campbell told him.

"I think we have to tread warily here," Raymond Adam told them both. "If we muck up this enquiry by rushing in feet-first the men in Kent and Surrey could lose out on any mistakes we make. There will not be a post mortem until early next week, Monday, I hope. In the meantime, we do nothing to spook this guy."

"The Letherford School team will be looking at miles of CCTV tape, any harm in giving them details of this silver car?" Fleming proposed. Adam thought about that and could visualise the difficulties later if he withheld it. "I'll call Jim Barrowman."

The following day was quiet and not just because it was Sunday. There was rain for the first time in a while.

The body of Morton Grant would be taken from the local mortuary to the mortuary of the larger general hospital at Paisley the next day where post-mortem examination was booked for Monday afternoon.

The Sunday had dragged a bit and Fleming was glad to get finished and go home. After dinner he spent time reading through the newspaper copies that Anthony and he had copied at the library. From the news reports of the time, Fleming made notes drawing up an involvement of people he had never heard of before, Harvey Johns and his wife, Cynthia Jane Ascot or Johns. Cynthia Johns had once been a pupil of the Mary Upton School, the school where her husband later became a science teacher. The same school where allegations had been made of the sexual molesting of young schoolgirls by schoolteacher Harvey Johns.

There seemed to be nothing specific in terms of relevance from the 1972 articles and entries but one coincidence caught Fleming's attention. Cynthia Johns had chosen the last day of the school year to commit suicide.

FIVE

As the sun rose over Loch Lomond that morning two anglers were retrieving their bottle traps from a small feeder burn leading into the loch. They had a total of eleven minnows which could be used later in the day as bait to fish for trout. Walking back towards the lochside car park, one of the fishermen pointed to a small shoe lying on its side on the shingle of the shore.

"Look at that, Jock. Some bairn has lost a shoe."

The man trod cautiously towards the water's edge and lifted the black shoe from the water. He looked inside and saw a smudged name written on the instep. It was too difficult to read but further inside there was something else. He probed with his fingers and pulled out a crushed sock. He opened out the sock and found a small label sewn onto it.

"Here Jock, see if you can make that out, your eyes are better than mine."

The other man studied the label and made out the name 'William J. Faraday'.

"That's the name o' that missing laddie, Jock. We'd be better tae tell the polis."

THE TALE OF THE OLD SCHOOL TIES

For judicial purposes of continuity, the nightshift officer from Friday night in Corran Bay accompanied the body of Morton Grant to Paisley for a two-doctor post-mortem examination.

As the hearse was being driven down the west side of Loch Lomond the police officer noticed that a police underwater search team were operating just south of the large car park.

The pathologists at Paisley determined that the three massive head wounds to the crown and back of Morton's head had been the cause of death. They had led to serious blood loss onto and down the man's back. This was consistent with the body being in an upright position when the wounds were sustained and not lying in the position in which he had been found and photographed, lying beside the railway track. There were facial injuries to the face, cheek, forehead, nose and chin, all consistent with striking his face on the road metal beside the track after death had occurred. The same was true of post-mortem bruising to the chest.

The injuries causing death had been inflicted by blows to the crown and back of the skull using a heavy blunt object, possibly a hammer. These wounds, though deep, contained no foreign matter. The facial injuries had traces of dirt and dust.

If Morton Grant had fallen headfirst but alive onto the track or the adjacent ground then the impact would have been absorbed by the body in line with that impact. In these circumstances the pathologists would expect to find consistent damage to the vertebra and the nature of the cranial damage would be quite different. There was no possibility of the wounds being self-inflicted, this had been an assault with fatal injury.

The clothing removed from the deceased had been transferred to the forensic laboratory for examination.

The pathologists had jointly contacted the Procurator Fiscal to inform him of their findings. The Fiscal called Raymond Adam and, while he was on the line, learned from Raymond Adam that a child's sock and shoe had been found on the west shore of Loch Lomond. The name tag had shown the sock to belong to William J. Faraday. The missing schoolboy from Kent could now be credibly linked to Scotland. Adams asked the Procurator Fiscal if they could now move against Bert Jones.

"Everything that you have is not pointing directly to Jones, Chief Inspector, any more than it is to anyone in this area. I accept that you feel that Jones is your man but I will require more than parti pris, I will need proof, absolute personal proof."

Raymond Adam put down his phone disconsolately.

"What the hell is parti pris?"

Valetta Johns was sewing by the light of a lamp as Mary Ainsworth polished the ornamental animals from the mantelpiece above the broad fireplace. The ladies had been discussing and reminiscing the war days and how

THE TALE OF THE OLD SCHOOL TIES

people had coped with various difficulties in everyday life when they were interrupted by a gentle knock to the front door. Mary Ainsworth went to answer it.

A young woman in her mid-twenties stood at the doorstep and asked for Mrs Johns.

"Come in," Mary said pleasantly. "Mrs Johns is through here."

Valetta Johns did not recognise the young woman.

"Do I know you?" she asked, aware of her own poor memory for faces.

"In a way, I expect that you will certainly know me, Mrs Johns. I am Sophie Rinstead. Lorna Templeton and I were girls.."

"You were the girls who ruined my son's career." Mrs Johns said, making no attempt to conceal her annoyance. "What do you hope to achieve by coming here to my house?"

"I am looking for your son to make my apologies," Sophie Rinstead said quietly. "Lorna and I were telling lies."

"It's rather late to be apologising now, Miss Rinstead. Anyway, where is this Lorna what's-her-name? Isn't she with you?"

"Lorna Templeton. She has gone to live in Australia." Sophie replied. "I cannot apologise for Lorna but I can tell you that we were both lying when we said that Mr Johns had molested us."

"Why did you lie about him in the first place?" a frosty-faced Valetta asked.

"He kept us back after school, Lorna and me. We had been doing something in class, giggling I think, so he made us stay behind and do a punishment exercise. He watched us the whole time and we giggled again. That made him really mad and wild. He came charging at us with a cane and I was sure he was going to attack us. He looked ready to strike me but he struck my desk instead and broke his cane. It was really frightening. We told the other girls afterwards and they suggested getting revenge on him by accusing him of indecently assaulting us. Some suggested rape but that was just ridiculous. We all felt that any other form of complaint would not be listened to and rumours went round the school without Lorna or me starting them. Our form mistress came to us and said that if these rumours were true then we must report them properly. We had to tell her exactly what Mr Johns had done to us during the punishment period. She had already heard from other girls what was being suggested."

Mrs Johns was nodding in recognition of how this matter had developed but her face remained stern and eyes were as cold as before.

"We began by telling how Mr Johns had really behaved but she pressed us for more. If we had said there was nothing more to tell she would have taken no action against the teacher but the other girls might have been suspended or even expelled for things they had said amounting to false accusations against Mr Johns. We both claimed that he had handled us over our breasts and put his hand up our

THE TALE OF THE OLD SCHOOL TIES

skirts." the young woman said, beginning to cry. She shook her head as she wiped her tears. "He never did that."

"And after that you were committed to your lies." Valetta Johns said with a further nod of her head. "Why tell me this now?"

"Lorna and I have been trying to find Mr Johns but Lorna has gone to Australia and I am continuing to look for him on my own to apologise." she explained as she still wept. "But nobody knows where he is."

"Neither do I know where he is." Valetta Johns said firmly and critically. I have never heard from him since these dark days. You do know that his poor wife hung herself over that carry-on?"

Sophie Rinstead held her handkerchief over her face and nodded.

"If you wish to apologise to my son, Miss Rinstead, you must find him first. You won't find him here, I can promise you that."

Mary Ainsworth placed an arm around the shoulders of Sophie Rinstead and ushered her towards the door. The young woman kept saying softly that she was 'sorry'.

"You didn't miss her." Mary remarked as she returned from seeing Sophie out.

"No, I didn't, did I? But now I can see how this happened. Harvey could lose the place too easily. That was always a problem with him." Valetta said slowly as if explaining something of what Sophie Rinstead had described.

Detective Sergeant Campbell and Detective Constable Darren Black entered the marine laboratory and asked to speak with the person in charge. They were invited into an office where they met Mark Goodfellow, the Chief Operational Executive.

"How can I help you, gentlemen?"

"Do you have someone working here by the name of Bert Jones?" Campbell asked, knowing that the answer should be affirmative. He had followed the silver car from Heather Road to the laboratory car park that morning and it was still sitting there now.

"Yes, we have a lab technician of that name. Do you want to speak to him?" Goodfellow asked.

"No, we don't, not yet at least, Mr Goodfellow. For the moment I would prefer to speak to you about him. What do you know about this man?"

"Well, he came here about four years ago from somewhere in the West Midlands." Mark Goodfellow said as he walked to a filing cabinet and drew a file. He was opening the file as he returned to his desk. "He had a fairly recent qualification, as I remember, but he has proved to be more academic scientifically than any of us expected from this record. He could have been a lab technician, or more, just about anywhere. I recall asking him why he chose to come here to Scotland to work when he had never been north of the border before. He told me that he had lost a dear friend quite suddenly and he had come north to put that behind him."

Campbell and Black exchanged glances.

"Do you have his qualification there and any other forms of identification?" Campbell asked.

"Yes, here you are, or a copy of it, which means that we saw the original."

"University of Manchester," Campbell read aloud. "BSc Life Sciences – Marine Biology, 6th June 1978. How long would that course have taken?"

"I asked the same question, Sergeant, because it showed me the extent of his available time. He said it took him four years because he needed to work manually to support himself."

"Doing what?" Campbell pressed.

"I think he said he worked as a mortuary assistant at a hospital but we never took the subject further. Here is his original application form for his current job."

Campbell took the form and copied what had been answered on the form. "I see he was already residing at 24 Heather Road when he applied here."

"Yes. He was in accommodation." Goodfellow confirmed.

"Do you have a National Insurance Number for him?"

"Yes, there you are"

Campbell copied the number.

"Thank you, Mr Goodfellow, you have been very helpful. I think we can leave Mr Jones alone for the moment. In fact, don't even mention that we asked about him."

Mark Goodfellow took this to mean that Jones was no longer of interest to the CID and he felt relieved to see them go.

As Campbell and Black returned to their car, Darren Black said quietly, "Don't look now, Dougie, but the Ford's gone."

"There could be a perfectly innocent reason for that," Campbell said as he unlocked the CID car, but he did not sound convincing.

Sophie Rinstead stood nervously on the stone doorstep of the large thatched house in Wiltshire. As she waited for a reply to her knocking, her anxiety was only exceeded by her determination. Lorna Templeton had been remorseful too, but Lorna had lacked the resolve to address her past sins in the way that Sophie Rinstead felt obliged to do. Now that Lorna had gone to Australia, Sophie felt released to act alone.

The door was opened by an elderly lady whose hair and clothing reflected a daily care and attention to her own appearance.

"Good morning, can I help you?" the older woman asked as one accustomed to the question.

"I want to speak to Mrs Ascot, is that you?"

"Yes, that is me, but who are you?"

"My name is Sophie Rinstead, Mrs Ascot. I have come to make my apologies." Sophie confessed.

The older lady looked to her left and right as if checking for something that Sophie should be apologising for.

"Then perhaps you would be better to come in, my dear, although I have no idea what you have to be apologising for." Mrs Ascot said, opening the door wider to allow Sophie to enter. She closed the door and ushered her guest into her large front sitting room where the armchairs and sofa were covered with floral loose covers. Like the other furnishings they spoke of wealth and a fondness for an earlier time. "Rinstead you said, I have heard that name before." Mrs Ascot said as if struggling with her own memory rather than any relevance to her visitor. "Please sit down."

"You might be remembering my name from ten years ago, Mrs Ascot. Sophie Rinstead and Lorna Templeton?" she posed, looking for recognition from her host. Mrs Ascot was still shaking her head but it was occurring to her that ten years ago would have made Sophie a schoolgirl.

"Were you and the other girl not at school then?" she suggested.

"We were both senior girls at Mary Upton." Sophie said, expecting to spark a bitter reaction.

"Oh, I see and what have you to apologise for?" Mrs Ascot asked, obviously failing to make the connection.

"Lorna Templeton and I told lies about your son-in-law, Harvey Johns, our science teacher. We both claimed to have been molested by him and he got the sack."

"Oh, I see, my dear and are you telling me now that you were not molested by him?" Mrs Ascot asked, sounding disappointed more than angry. "Those of us who knew Harvey were not at all surprised to hear of your allegations. He was a dangerous unpredictable man, not at all suited to teaching. I was in teaching, so was my daughter, Cynthia. If she had not been so stubborn and loyal, I would have told Mary Upton School to have looked twice at Harvey Johns."

"But he never actually molested us like we said," Sophie protested. "He only ran at us and hit my desk with a cane. He didn't strike us, he just scared us."

"Did he seem to be acting in an appropriate manner for a teacher of young girls at that moment?" Mrs Ascot asked rhetorically.

"No, we didn't think so. He really scared us. That is why we lied about him, to get our own back, so to speak."

"So ten years ago you accused him falsely of sexually molesting you when you were perfectly entitled to be reporting him for what he actually did, a violent outburst." Mrs Ascot said frankly. "What makes you think you are due me an apology?"

"Because he lost his job. The story was in the papers and your daughter, his wife, took her own life." Sophie said in explanation, her voice cracking and protesting at her need to explain.

Mrs Ascot's head dropped forward onto her open hands. She remained like that in silence for a few moments before looking up at Sophie.

"Forgive me, my dear, you have been living under the impression that your allegations brought the shame and disgrace which drove Cynthia to take her own life. That supposition was broadly expressed in the newspapers too, but it simply was not true. Cynthia had been learning through a series of frightening experiences, similar to your own, and worse, just what kind of man she had married. Her father, God rest him, implored her to get out of that marriage for her own safety but she was stubborn as I have told you. Her husband left Mary Upton, as you know and applied immediately for a position at a boys' school. He was turned down to nobody's surprise but his own. He was actually surprised and raging mad. Everybody had it in for him, Mary Upton, the boys' school, Cynthia, everyone was at fault for his shortcomings but him. Cynthia finally stood up to him and demanded a divorce. He was incensed. More rejection, you see. He just could not handle it, he was such a narcissist that he couldn't understand being rejected. He would not be disgraced by any divorce, that's what he told her. She reminded him that he had already disgraced his own name by his own deeds. He said that no-one in their right mind would believe anything said against him and he was not going to have people talking behind his back just because his wife wanted to divorce him."

"So, did this push Cynthia into suicide?" Sophie asked, sounding sympathetic and understanding.

"For me the answer to that question is 'no'. The circumstances suggest that it did, I agree, but I blame her death in every respect, on Harvey Johns. Cynthia was two months pregnant when she died. She never told him that. He was unemployed and would have blamed her for being pregnant. She wanted away, yes. She would have left him but she knew that he would pursue her. She felt trapped, I can see that, but it was never in her nature to take her own life. I still do not believe it. Even the policeman who told me about it said that he was surprised how she had climbed over the balustrade with a sheet round her neck. The balustrade was almost as tall as her."

"Do you think he did it?" Sophie asked with her eyes wide open.

"I think he is capable of doing it, yes certainly, but he was apparently somewhere else at the time." Mrs Ascot said. "So, you see Miss Rinstead, you should not feel too much remorse for your lies. Among normal people, your teenage emotions are recognisable, wrong but recognisable. Harvey Johns on the other hand is anything but normal. You and the other girl never caused Cynthia's death, he did, whether he was there at the time or not."

"She must have loved him at one time." Sophie suggested.

"Of course, but Cynthia never made sure that he felt the same, or was even capable of feeling the same. By the time she found his true character, they were already married. Before the marriage he behaved with what we all took to be normal happiness. Now we know it was pride in the thought of someone being attracted by him. After the marriage it was all about him and Cynthia had become property, or a trophy of some kind. We all have to face adversity and we all make mistakes but not Harvey Johns, nothing would ever be his mistake, he would never accept the blame for anything. He simply expected to receive everything and anything he wanted. He was an impossible man for my daughter to live with."

"Cynthia died on the last day of the school year, Mrs Ascot. Was there any significance to that?"

"Cynthia would not be aware of the date. I do not know if it was simply coincidence but to have Cynthia die on that date would be more typical of his behaviour. She was not one to make statements but he certainly was. He always did things in a way that seemed more sensational than they deserved. If he did something that others had done then his version would require to carry an added significance. I hope there is nothing significant about the date but you have me wondering now."

"What does he do nowadays?" Sophie asked.

"I have no idea. After Cynthia died, he got insurance money, I know that. He sold the house and went away. Somebody told me that he had gone to Manchester but frankly, I was not interested."

"You didn't like him. Did he ever threaten you?" Sophie asked cautiously.

"No dear, I cannot say that. He was not pleasant but he never threatened me. He did kill my cat, though, I am pretty sure of that but I could never prove it." Mrs Ascot remembered.

"How did he do that?" Sophie asked with that wide-eyed look again.

"He chopped off her head and legs dear. He left her like that for me to find," Mrs Ascot said. "He denied it of course."

"What a terrible thing to do." Sophie sounded disgusted. "I don't really feel like apologising to someone who could do that. Was Cynthia buried?"

"Yes she was. She lies buried next to her dad. I know she would have liked that although she was much too young to be thinking about such things."

"Is she buried in the graveyard beside the church?" Sophie enquired, her finger pointing in the general direction of the church she had passed.

"Yes dear, in the aisle parallel to the back wall." Mrs Ascot replied, guessing at her visitor's intentions.

"I had better go now, Mrs Ascot, but it has been a real pleasure to meet you and to hear some home truths. I see things differently now. I do not need to go farther than the graveyard to make my apologies."

"You are a fine young woman, my dear. You must be careful to avoid the Harvey Johns of this world. Feel free to return for a visit any time you wish to, you will be welcome."

Douglas Campbell sat at his desk feeling uneasy about the departure of Bert Jones from the laboratory. He was considering a telephone call to Mark Goodfellow when his telephone rang. It was Mark Goodfellow.

"Sergeant Campbell, I felt that I should call you, Bert Jones left the laboratory this morning after seeing you come in. He was in a hurry and muttered something about being late for a doctor's appointment. He has not returned or phoned in."

"Right, Mr Goodfellow, if he should do either of these things please let me know. I'll check at his house. Thanks for the call." Campbell put the phone down and turned to his colleague.

"Darren, phone round the surgeries and ask if Bert Jones had an appointment at any of them this morning. I'm going to Heather Road to see if he is at home. If he is I'll get you and a couple of the boys to join me up there. The man is probably miles away but we would be better to be sure of our facts before I phone Raymond Adam"

When Campbell drew up outside number twenty-four it was obvious that the silver car was not there. The door serving the upstairs flat was in the end of the building, with front and back doors serving the ground floor flat. Campbell tried Jones' door and found it locked by a Yale lock. He went round the back of the building to where the two dustbins sat side by side in the sunlight. Campbell noticed a spray pattern of dark spots in the roughcast above the bins with some similar spots on the outside of both bins. He lifted the lids of both bins and saw that one contained neatly wrapped black polythene parcels tied with string, as described by Fleming. The other bin had loose everyday items of domestic waste. Being alone for the time being, Campbell left things as they were, waiting until he had spoken to Raymond Adam.

The end of the working day saw neither the return of Bert Jones to his home nor to his place of employment. A lookout was circulated for the silver Ford. Campbell and Black returned to 24 Heather Road to photograph the area and specifically the spots on the wall and dustbins. On Raymond Adam's instructions they took possession of both the dustbins. Both had possible blood spatter on the outside and Bert Jones had access to both, even if the neighbour's bin looked free of evidence internally. They would both go to the forensic laboratory as they were. Adam would phone the council cleansing department and arrange replacements for the convenience of the neighbour and any future tenant of Number 24. The CID lifted samples of the spots on the roughcast wall and from the outside of both bins to have them examined for human blood.

When Fleming began nightshift he heard of the day's developments and of the on-going debate among the CID as to whether a search warrant should be executed for 24 Heather Road when neither Bert Jones nor any legal representative could be present.

"The house is rented." Fleming reminded Campbell. "Why not see if the owners, the Housing Association, can supply two officials to be present as independent observers?"

Leaving the CID to debate further, Fleming took

THE TALE OF THE OLD SCHOOL TIES

Hamish MacLeod up to 24 Heather Road and went round to the rear of the building. By the light of their torches the men saw the spots in the roughcast as referred to by Campbell. Fleming looked closely at the ground behind where the bins had sat.

The back door of the ground floor flat opened and an old man in a dressing gown stood in the doorway, shining a torch towards the police officers.

"You boys back again?" he said, sounding relieved that it had not been anyone else.

"Yes sir," Fleming replied, "Nothing to worry about, we are just looking around this bit here where the bins were sitting. The CID took your bins away but did they look at the ground?"

"I've no idea," the old man said looking puzzled. "They took my bin away but I am supposed to be getting a new one. Some bugger was at my bin on Friday or Saturday night. They left a dirty hand mark on the lid. I washed it off on Sunday."

"What colour was it, this mark? Could it have been blood?" Fleming asked.

"It could have been, I suppose, but I am colour blind. I can't be sure." the older man said.

Fleming had brought a bag from the office along with rubber gloves. Hamish held the bag open while Fleming picked up the bits and pieces from the ground between the position of the bins and the back wall of the house, an area that had received little attention until now. The old man stood at his door and watched. He was Mr Tom Gray, he told them.

"Did you know the man upstairs?" Fleming asked Mr Tom Gray.

"In the past four years we have hardly said more than 'Hello'. He works at that marine place, that's all I know about him"

"He doesn't work weekends, does he? What does he do then?" Fleming asked as he picked items up for examination. "He has been away at weekends but he is usually here. He goes out to the shops but he is never away too long." Mr Gray replied.

"Was he not out on Friday night?" Fleming asked.

"Yes, he was. He seemed to take something to the dump. Late on, after midnight." Tom Gray speculated.

"What made you think that?" Fleming asked.

"I had gone to bed and it was after midnight for the boxing on the television kept me up 'til then. I was just about asleep when I heard him out at the bins. It sounded like he was trying to put something into the bins but it was too big for that so he dragged whatever he had to his car and then the motor went away. I've no idea when he came back but the sound of water running through the pipes woke me up about three. He must have been running a bath or something. I went back to sleep."

"Was it daylight at three, when you woke?"

"Yes. I could see the light through my curtains, 'course I never got up."

"Thank you Mr Gray. We are keeping you from your bed. I'm sorry for that. We will be on our way now."

As they walked back to their car Hamish asked why the old man hadn't spoken up earlier.

"I'm guessing that nobody asked him." Fleming said as he stopped beside the lamp post at the kerb.

"This pole has just been painted, Hamish. See how clean and glossy it is?"

"Yes, you're right," Hamish answered failing to see a significance. Fleming kept his thoughts to himself and continued their previous conversation. "You heard Mr Gray's explanation of Friday night's events. It fits what we know, but the old man has no reason for suspecting Jones of doing anything criminal so why would he report what he heard?"

Mary Ainsworth walked up the front steps towards Valetta Johns' front door with no concerns other than keeping her home baked sponge cake level in her basket. Mrs Johns had no particular liking for cake but the occasional double cream sandwich was always welcomed for the effort and 'special treat' of Mary's cakes.

She put her key in the lock and unlocked the door before depressing the handle and pushing the door with her body weight. The door would only open by twelve to fourteen inches. Realising that something was terribly wrong, Mary placed her basket and handbag down on the doorstep and pushed her head round the door to see the body of Valetta Vivien Johns lying motionless behind it. She pushed the door a little harder, moving Mrs Johns as she did so, but this allowed her to gain access to the house and the telephone. She felt Mrs Johns' neck for a pulse and thought she could detect a weak pulse in the otherwise unconscious and pale old lady. She dialled the emergency number and requested an ambulance immediately.

She gently eased Mrs Johns in a direction that took her away from the door and then settled her into the recovery position. There was bruising visible on Valetta's face and legs. Her walking stick still lay on the staircase. She was dressed in her nightdress and her body felt cold. Mary brought a quilted cover from the sitting room. It was one that Valetta would occasionally use to cover her legs while sitting on colder days at home. While fetching this cover Mary noticed that the doors to the patio were open. After covering Mrs Johns she went back to close and lock the French doors.

When the ambulance crew arrived they quickly placed an oxygen mask over Valetta's mouth and nose before easing her gently onto a stretcher. Mary Ainsworth lifted the walking stick and pulled the front door behind her securing it by the Yale lock. She accompanied Valetta to hospital and explained to the ambulance man how Mrs Johns had probably fallen downstairs during the night. She may having been going to the toilet but she was not good on her feet due to her arthritis.

Mary was permitted to stay and to sit close to her

friend while staff constantly monitored Mrs Johns' condition. Their patient remained unconscious but Mary imagined that the colour was gradually returning to Valetta's complexion.

Mary eventually gave in to nurses' encouragement to go for something to eat at the canteen. When she returned to the bedside she found that the mask had been taken from Valetta's face and the monitor was displaying fewer settings. The window had been opened, making the room less stuffy. Mary moved closer and took Valetta's frail hand. It felt cold so she continued to hold it loosely. There was an occasional brief visit from a nurse but otherwise the room was left to Mary and Valetta. Mary began to relax, her head falling back against the wing of her chair.

She awoke midway through the afternoon, the clock on the wall read two-thirty and Valetta was squeezing her hand.

"You are awake, Mrs Johns." Mary said, as if to herself.

"I am awake Mary but I am sore all over. Is there any water here?"

Mary rose immediately and went to the water jug and glass on the cabinet.

"Here you are my dear, just little sips would be best. These masks make one's throat dry, I know." Mary tilted the glass with one hand while supporting Mrs Johns' head with the other to allow the older woman to take enough water to wet her mouth. At that she was satisfied.

"Where are we, Mary?" the lady asked in less of a whisper.

"We are at St. Joseph's Hospital, Mrs Johns. You fell down your stairs at home, don't you remember?"

Valetta Johns stared straight ahead of her, at nothing in particular, a pose she often adopted when trying to recall events.

"I do not think that I fell, Mary." she said finally. "Did you find me in the morning? Is that what happened?"

"Yes dear, you were lying behind your front door, unconscious and ever so cold."

"There was a draught you know. That is why I got up from bed, there was a draught in the house." the elderly lady said as if recalling slowly a memory of the previous night.

"I will go to the house and check how things are. I never had time this morning." Mary assured her.

The older woman's eyes opened wide and she spoke as forcefully as her strength would allow. "No Mary, don't go there, not on your own. It isn't safe."

Her impassioned advice had lifted her from her pillow and now she fell backwards looking exhausted. Mary rose to inform the nursing staff that their patient was now awake. She felt foolish when she returned with a nurse to find Valetta asleep once more. The nurse smiled at the situation.

Mrs Johns obviously needs rest. We would be best to allow her to sleep as she feels like it." the nurse said quietly. "I'll let the doctor know that she woke up and you gave her some water, I see."

"Yes, a sip or two. Her mouth was dry."

"We may be putting the mask back on later. You can expect a dry throat from it. In the meantime you might be as well to leave her and come back at the evening visiting. It is from 7 until 9p.m."

"Thank you, nurse. I will be back. Be sure to tell her that if she wakes up again. She relies on me."

Undaunted by Valetta's concerns for her safety, Mary Ainsworth headed back to her friend's house. When she opened the front door she found a message written on a sealed envelope asking Mrs Johns to call a Graeme Benson at a given number. She called the number and found herself connected to the council offices. She asked for Graeme Benson and was put through.

"Graeme Benson, how can I help?"

"Mr Benson, this is not Mrs Johns but it is her housekeeper, Mary Ainsworth. Mrs Johns has had an accident and is in hospital, quite ill. Is there anything I can do for you?"

"I am sorry to hear that, Mrs Ainsworth. I am employed in the department of the council which deals with parks and cemeteries. My cemetery foreman has contacted me today to tell me that his men went to the cemetery this morning to cut the grass and they discovered damage done to the headstone of the late Brigadier Wesley Johns."

"Oh dear, what kind of damage?" Mary asked

anxiously, remembering the beautiful black marble headstone she had taken Valetta to visit so often.

"I am afraid it has been totally destroyed, smashed into pieces quite deliberately by some mindless individual."

"Has there been much of that kind of thing happening in the cemetery, Mr Benson?"

"No, Mrs Ainsworth, in fact this is the first malicious damage in that cemetery for years. It seems strange that no other headstones appear to have been touched, just this one. I should report the matter to the police if I were you. You can refer them to me if you wish. This was no accident. Be sure to inform Mrs Johns, she is the owner of the headstone and it may even be covered by insurance."

"Thank you, Mr Benson." Mary Ainsworth said quietly, suddenly remembering the warning Valetta had given her so earnestly. She lifted her basket and handbag, listened for a moment, heard nothing and left.

SIX

With Bert Jones on the loose and running from the law, Raymond Adam wanted some indication of where the fugitive might go. He spoke directly to Mark Goodfellow and heard of the qualification gained at Manchester University in 1978. He also heard that Jones had supposedly worked at a general hospital in that area to support himself during his studies. Presumably the employment had stopped once the degree was obtained and he had moved north. It wasn't much but it was something. Raymond Adam thanked Goodfellow and asked him to report any call or correspondence he might receive from Jones.

His telephone was no sooner replaced than it rang again. This was the forensic lab to inform him that while emptying the items from the dustbin belonging to Thomas Gray of Heather Road, Jones' downstairs neighbour, they had found a heavily blood-stained ballpeen hammer wrapped in newspaper and stuffed inside an empty cereal carton. Examination was yet to be carried out but this looked very much like a murder weapon.

On the stroke of 7 p.m. Mary Ainsworth entered the room occupied by Valetta Johns to find the older lady sitting up in bed, quite awake.

"Oh Mary, I am so glad to see you. I can only imagine the day that you have had. Sit down, dear, I am feeling much better now."

"I don't suppose you want any of this cream sponge. I brought it this morning and I've been carrying it about all day." Mary said with a smile as she lifted the cake out of its tin container.

"Leave it there. Perhaps the nurses will share with me at supper time. Tell me how things went today. I hope you never went near the house." Valetta said.

"I only checked for mail, Mrs Johns, but there wasn't any mail. There was a note from the council to contact them and I did. It seems that there has been some vandalism in the cemetery. Brigadier Johns' headstone has been damaged."

"Smashed to pieces?" Valetta suggested as if she knew what to expect.

"Yes dear, how did you know?"

"I didn't." Valetta said. "But I feared the worst. Never mind. It will be fixed, or at least I shall order a replacement."

"The council man said to report the matter to the police." Mary told her.

"You haven't done that, have you?" Valetta asked seriously.

"Not yet." Mary replied. "It is for you to decide, as the council man said, it is your headstone."

"Never mind the police. I will order a new one." Valetta said in the manner of one stating her last word on the issue. "They come round with tea after the visiting. I will have my cake then, Mary. It was very good of you."

"Has anyone suggested when you might get home?" Mary asked.

"No. They do not really know that yet but I have given them your home number. I hope you don't mind but if I was getting out I would want you to know about it. They have promised to tell you in good time."

"You are not worried about returning home are you?" Mary asked cautiously.

"I will be going home by ambulance, Mary. Why should I worry?"

Mary took this to mean that Valetta expected the company of ambulance personnel when she entered her home. She would also want the company of Mary herself when these ambulance people left.

"You are not in a hurry to go home, are you?" Mary suggested.

"Not really. I ought to be safe here and it will give you a bit of a break, Mary."

"I will be happier knowing you are here. It would be safer, as you say."

Anthony Halbooth walked into town, to the library, after receiving a call from Mrs Campbell. His ordered books had arrived. She smiled when she saw him and reached beneath the counter for two new volumes of Roman poetry.

"Did you hear about our murder?" Mrs Campbell asked, her face solemn but her voice as soft as usual.

"No. What murder? Here in Corran Bay?" Anthony replied.

"Yes. Morton Grant was murdered. Remember the man who held the door open for you the last time you came here for books?"

"Vaguely," Anthony said. "Was that Morton Grant?"

"Yes, that was Morton. He worked for the council as a painter." Mrs Campbell explained, knowing that Anthony actually knew very few people.

"Who would do that?" Anthony wondered.

"They say it was some man that works at the lab. That's just gossip, mind you, somebody called Bert Jones. I've never heard of him."

"Did Mr Grant have any family?" Anthony asked.

"Not that I know of," Mrs Campbell answered. "He was a bachelor and that gives me a bit of a problem, I suppose." Mrs Campbell said thoughtfully. "Morton had books to return. If you see Andrew Fleming before I do you could mention it to him Anthony."

"I will if I can." Anthony promised.

Detective Sergeant Ken Dibley felt that he was being sent on a wild goose chase to find a 'Bert Jones' who had graduated from Manchester University with a degree in marine biology in June 1978. Once he found a friendly records assistant life became much easier.

"That would be 'life sciences' with a field study in the first year and a laboratory study in the final year." the young girl said cheerily as she turned a carousel of index cards. "Quite a few Jones' I'm afraid. Bert would be Robert?"

"Bert is what I have but you are probably right." Dibley said as if any difficulty would not be his fault.

"Ah, here it is. Normally I would expect to find Robert or Herbert but this guy really is under Bert H. Jones." the girl said triumphantly. "Now 5778/FLS/1978, where are you?"

She pulled a file that listed graduates from Life Sciences in 1978. For each graduate there was a summary of their achievements during the course together with a brief character assessment.

"It says here that he was an intensely personal individual who nevertheless performed well with consummate ease as if pre-disposed to the work involved. He is distinctly lacking in humour and occasionally in etiquette but his industry cannot be faulted. He was employed in a non-medical role at Valley Tudinar Hospital to subsist during study. Does that help?"

"Does it give an address or some sort of reference for him?" Dibley asked.

"No. I guess he doesn't owe us any money." the girl said, smiling to herself as she replaced the file.

"I hope I get more at the hospital." Dibley said with no discernible smile. "But thank you."

Mary Ainsworth was worried by recent events. She was worried because her dear friend and employer was worried, if not actually scared, despite the display of bravado. Mary decided to speak to the police about her concerns. Surely she could do that without formally reporting anything?"

A young police officer listened patiently to all that she said and asked if Mary wanted to report the damage to the headstone.

"It's not really my place to report it and Mrs Johns has told me not to do so but she is afraid of something." Mary blurted out, trying to make her positon clear.

"But if she is not reporting the malicious damage to the headstone then what can we do to help you?" the young man asked.

"I don't know, really." Mary answered a little pathetically.

A crime prevention sergeant who had been listening to the conversation while writing on a form stopped and looked up at Mary.

"Could she be worried about her house, with her being away in hospital?"

"She is concerned about her house, yes. In fact she is worried about me going to her house on my own. I do not know why, I have been going there for the past four years. She has not been worried like this before."

The sergeant tossed the form into a wire tray and told Mary, "Come on, lass. I'll take you round there and maybe we can see what she is worried about."

With a nod to the young officer, he put on his jacket and hat and left with Mary for Valetta Johns' home. On the way he asked Mary about family members and troublesome neighbours but Mary was not in a position to comment on either. Mr Johns had been a brigadier and he had died five years earlier. She had not known him but she had taken Valetta to visit his grave many times. She knew of nobody with a wish to break up the man's gravestone.

When they reached the house Mary unlocked the door and went in, extremely glad to have the sergeant's company. She showed him through to the sitting room and explained to him that the French doors to the patio had been open that morning. Mrs Johns had felt the draught and had risen from her bed to investigate. She had then fallen down the stairs.

The sergeant crossed to the doors and stopped to look at a spot of mud on the carpet.

"Was that there before?" he asked.

"Not when I was here. I dare say Mrs Johns could have brought it in with her. She goes out to leave food for the birds, you see. That's probably when she forgot to lock these doors behind her." Mary supposed.

The sergeant studied the locking mechanism for the PVC doors. They were locked from the inside by turning a latch that operated three bars in an 'L' shape. These fitted into grooves on the opposite door and when engaged, made the door secure. There was no way to lock or unlock the doors from the outside where the handle was only useful if the doors were already unlocked. With no sign of damage Mary had to be right about Mrs Johns failing to lock the doors.

"If the doors are locked then no wind would ever affect them but if they are not locked then a wind can push them open," Mary informed him. The sergeant seemed reassured.

"Let's check the rest of the house shall we?"

They went around the lower rooms and saw nothing untoward. They then went upstairs with the sergeant taking time to look at the width of the treads and stability of the handrail.

"This is Mrs Johns' bedroom." Mary said as they saw another room with nothing out of place except the duvet cover lifted to one side as Mrs Johns had risen to investigate the draught. Mary was staring at the bedside cabinet on the far side of the bed.

"I wonder what she did with her husband's photograph?" she said quietly. "It has always been on top of that side cabinet. I dust in here every day and I have never known her to move it before."

"It does not sound like something that would be of value to anyone else." the sergeant remarked.

"No. That's true." Mary agreed.

THE TALE OF THE OLD SCHOOL TIES

They went into the bathroom on the left beyond the stairs and found nothing amiss. They then entered the second bedroom and Mary Ainsworth gasped.

"What's wrong?" the sergeant asked.

"That silk cover over the bed is all creased as if someone has been lying on it. It's never been like that." Mary said, obviously alarmed at the sight of a bed she had never known to be used.

The sergeant moved closer to the bed and noticed a small smear of mud near the bottom of the cover. "I don't suppose that this was there before, either?" he asked, pointing it out to Mary. Mary shook her head.

The sergeant now looked into a paper bin beside a writing table. It was empty apart from a framed 8 x 6 photograph of a military officer with an impressive array of medal ribbons. He lifted it out and showed it to Mary.

"The late husband?" he asked.

"Yes, that is the photograph from Mrs Johns' room. That's Brigadier Wesley Johns who died five years ago." Mary said, taking the photograph to return it to Mrs Johns' room.

The sergeant was opening wardrobe doors and cupboards.

"Mrs Johns has had a visitor but I don't think he was a thief. He hasn't actually taken anything as far as you can tell and what he has done appears to have been personal, the discarded photo frame and, possibly the damage to the headstone. Perhaps Mrs Johns has some thoughts on this person. Her fall may not have been an accident and she was warning you that it could be dangerous to come here alone, so you were telling me. I think we need to talk to Mrs Johns when she is well enough."

After checking the house thoroughly, with the exception of the inaccessible loft, the sergeant locked the patio doors and Mary took a few perishables from the fridge. He agreed with Mrs Johns that Mary would be better not to return until she was well enough. At that time she would be required to permit entry for a scenes of crime unit.

From a parked car across the street they were watched as they locked up and left.

The Valley Tudinar Hospital was not in his area so Detective Sergeant Dibley merely added his own actions and findings to the enquiry and passed it on to West Midlands for their attention.

Detective Sergeant Sally Armstrong of West Midlands Police continued the enquiry by attending at the hospital where Bert Jones was said to have worked. She knew that the hospital had changed hands and was now occupied by the NHS but prior to 1980 it had been in private ownership specialising in acute paediatric care. She found that records of personnel from the hospital's private days had been removed but she was advised to speak with some of the retained staff. Several nurses seemed to think that a Bert Jones had worked as a porter or mortuary assistant at one

THE TALE OF THE OLD SCHOOL TIES

time. She was prompted to speak to 'old Frank' at the mortuary.

Frank Dalton was not so old, in his mid-fifties, but he could remember Bert Jones

"He was a clever young man." Frank told Sally Armstrong. "Too clever to be working here in the mortuary, but then he was studying at the university. He never spoke much in here and all the time he was here, I don't think I ever saw him smile, not once. Very serious young man, very strange."

"What had he done before he came here?" Sally asked.

"He said he had worked for short spells in shops and the like, all short term work. There was some mix-up with his National Insurance but he got that sorted out eventually. It went on for a few weeks, him writing to them and them to him."

"Did he explain that problem to you?" Sally asked.

"Not really, he just said that they had his name wrong. Somebody had picked it up wrong somewhere. That's what he said."

"Was that before he went to university, Frank?"

"Yes, I believe it was."

"Isn't it a bit morbid working in a mortuary?" Sally asked, suggesting some sympathy for Frank.

"It was worse under the Valley Tudinar. It was mostly children back then. I felt sorry for every one of them kids. Us older folks, well it's inevitable, you know what I mean? But them kids." he said shaking his head.

"I suppose I do." Sally replied, suddenly feeling every day of her thirty-five years.

A search warrant had been obtained for 24 Heather Road and Raymond Adam attended to carry out the search in the company of Douglas Campbell, Darren Black and Fergus MacKinley, a Housing Inspector for the owners. Mr Gray came out from the bottom flat to see what was going on but disguised his interest by asking when his new bin was going to arrive. He recognised Campbell and Black.

"You boys are CID, aren't you? If you are going into that fellow's flat you maybe don't have to break in," he said, hoping to be helpful.

"What do you mean?" asked Douglas Campbell.

"I still have a spare key for that flat from the time old Mhairi stayed up there. I used to get her messages and her medicine for her before she died. I don't know if the lock is still the same but you could try my key" he turned as he spoke and went into his kitchen, returning with a Yale key. The police officers and the housing official exchanged smiles.

Mr Gray's key did unlock the door, saving the expense of damaging the property. Mr MacKinley explained to Tom Gray why the key could not be given back to him.

Inside the two bedroom flat there was nothing of much interest to the CID officers. The house was surprisingly clean and tidy for a single male occupant. The kitchen and

THE TALE OF THE OLD SCHOOL TIES

bathroom were both clinically clean, ominously so for men with forensic examination in mind. There was a stainless steel bin in the kitchen with a black plastic bin liner. The bag had contents which appeared at first glance to be no different from any other kitchen waste but Campbell was remembering how the ballpeen hammer had been secreted inside a cereal packet. He elected not to miss things as easily this time. He removed each item from the bag to be individually examined before placing it in the sink. He removed a small polythene bag of teabags, used kitchen roll, fruit cores and potato peelings and several napkin holders or something similar. He placed these into the sink and continued to carefully lift out the rest of the domestic waste until the bag was empty. The inner surface of the bin liner had not been soiled by the contents but there were white dust particles at the bottom, a lot of white dust particles. Dougie Campbell pointed this out to Raymond Adam and asked for his thoughts on the particles.

"Just leave this as it is for now, Dougie." the Detective Chief Inspector instructed. "Has anyone come across any tools so far?"

Darren Black had just opened a cupboard which held tins of food but on the floor of the cupboard was a single metal tray which held a small assortment of tools.

"Over here, sir."

"Well done, Darren, is that a hacksaw?" Raymond Adam asked.

Darren Black lifted the hacksaw with a gloved hand and handed it to his boss. The DCI looked at it closely before showing it to Campbell.

"The teeth of this saw still have small white deposits, Dougie. The dust in the bin bag has been caused by our man cutting something with this saw."

"Wait a minute," Campbell said with a show of inspiration. "Look at these rings in this bag. I thought they were napkin rings but who knows?"

He untied the clear polythene bag and took out one of the 'rings', handing it to Adam.

"It's just some sort of plaster and I can see tooth marks from the saw on it." Adam said with a suggestion of achievement. "But there is more than that. The outer surface of this ring has been written on. Get the rest of these rings out here, Dougie. Just lift them with your pinkie. They are going to the lab along with that saw and the bag with the white dust. Well done, boys."

The toolbox tray that may once have held a ballpeen hammer was also taken for forensic examination.

"Why would he keep brake fluid and toothpicks in the kitchen cupboard?" Darren asked, speaking to no-one in particular. Raymond Adam came across to look at the items mentioned. They sat on a shelf in distinct contrast to the other items.

"These used to be used to alter documents, MOT certificates, car insurance dates, that sort of thing, basically changing details on an otherwise valid document. We don't know if our man was at that game, do we?" Adam asked, suggesting that the toothpicks and brake fluid be left alone.

"That's something we haven't seen much of, official documents." Douglas Campbell remarked. "Maybe we need to look a bit harder."

As the CID officers continued their search of the upstairs flat without finding personal documents or anything else of interest, Mr Thomas Gray was standing outside his back door looking along his back wall. "Some bugger's away with my mash hammer." he muttered to himself.

"Someone has been in your house, Mrs Johns," the sergeant said emphatically. "You were afraid for Mary going there by herself, so you know that there was someone there."

"Oh dear," the old lady said wearily. "I suppose there was."

"And I suppose that you have an idea just who that someone was." the sergeant said firmly. "A personal scare for you in your own home and a singularly personal attack on your late husband's gravestone, who would this person be, Mrs Johns?"

The old lady looked defeated and helpless.

"Harvey," she said reluctantly.

"Who is Harvey?" the sergeant asked.

"My son, Harvey Johns," she said in little more than a

whisper. "Who else would destroy my husband's gravestone on his birthday?"

Anthony Halbooth sat reading quietly in the sitting room. It was Thursday afternoon and Gretchen had not been that day to attend to him. He had risen at eight that morning and had eaten only breakfast cereal and an apple. It was not yet two o'clock and Anthony was not at all aware of the time, indeed for the time being, he was two thousand three hundred years behind the clock as he soaked in the lyrical beauty of Roman poetry.

He was not expecting the arrival of a car in the courtyard behind him and when the vehicle stopped it was not immediately noticed by Anthony. He reached the door to the kitchen as the tall, slim figure of his father came through the rear door.

"Ah, you are here, Anthony." his father said as if surprised to see his son. "Mrs Moreno told me that you were in London."

"Yes, I was, but that was almost a fortnight ago," Anthony replied. "You were in America she told me."

"Were you looking for me?" his father asked. "Was something wrong?"

Anthony shook his head but avoided eye contact with his father.

"Did you notice that another boy had gone missing from Letherford School?" Anthony asked, turning now to look at his father.

THE TALE OF THE OLD SCHOOL TIES

"Yes, I heard from Mrs Moreno. A thing like that could ruin that school, I dare say." his father responded as he began to empty a small suitcase into the washing machine. "Gretchen comes tomorrow, am I right?"

"Yes, tomorrow morning."

"Good." his father said, moving away from the washing machine as if he had done all that was required of him where his own laundry was concerned. "Has mother been here at all?"

"She turned up for a couple of days but she has gone back to her dig," Anthony answered with as much interest as he had felt at the time.

"We had an infestation of bluebottles in the laundry room for a spell." Anthony said in the hope of drawing a response.

"My fault entirely." his father admitted immediately. "I left my butcher meat in there a while back. I forgot it at the time but then I realised there would be a problem."

"You dealt with it then?" Anthony said easily.

"Threw the lot out the other week when I was home for a talk to Commerce." his father said as if the affair had been no big deal. He obviously had just visited home to get rid of the rotten butcher meat and saw no reason to enter the house.

"You are the only one with a key." Anthony said saucily.

"Nonsense," his father said sternly. "The spare key hangs in the garage."

"Does anyone else actually know that, father?"

"Perhaps not." his father conceded. "But it is there nevertheless."

Anthony gave up.

"Are you home for long this time?" he asked as he returned to his book.

"Two whole weeks," the professor replied as if bored already.

"There has been a murder here in Corran Bay." Anthony told him. "A council worker called Morton Grant was murdered. The police seem to think that it was committed by a man called Bert Jones. Mrs Campbell at the library told me."

His father had been walking toward the stairs but stopped and looked down at his feet.

"Bert Jones, Bert Jones, why do I know that name?" he said to himself before finally shaking his head and proceeding to climb the stairs.

Andrew Fleming went into the supermarket with Mary but told her he would join her at the café. He told her that he was going to meet an old man in the town. He bought cigarettes and drove up to 24 Heather Road. Tom Gray was grateful for the cigarettes and the company.

Fleming explained that he could only stay half-an-hour at most but Fleming was night shift and Tom Gray was an early-bedder so this was the only suitable time for both of them to talk.

THE TALE OF THE OLD SCHOOL TIES

"You knew Morton Grant, didn't you, Tom?"

"Aye, since he was a wee boy. He was always a bit weird, but in a harmless way was Morton, he had a head full of broken glass but as I say, harmless."

"So you could not suggest anyone who might want to kill him?" Fleming said, more in statement than question.

"The man had no enemies, we all know that. He might have said or done something to offend a stranger, somebody that didnae know how to take him, but that wouldnae be reason to kill him, would it?" the old man said, shaking his head. "He was up here last week," Tom Gray said spontaneously as the memory occurred to him. "He was painting these lamp-posts out in the street. There is one right outside my house. I was watching him."

"Would Jones have been at home at that time?" Fleming asked.

"Aye he was. He was sawing something. I've heard him at that before."

"He's done a runner, did you know that?" Fleming asked, aware of the answer.

"Aye, the car's away. There was never police here for fifty years then they all arrive at once." the old man laughed. "I doubt I'll no be seeing the scientist again. Oh, I forgot to say to the CID men, but I think he has taken my mash hammer from the back wall out there."

"You sure it was Jones?" Fleming asked.

"Well it was there on Sunday and then missing on Monday, does that no seem like him?"

"Has Jones always had that silver car?" Fleming asked.

"All the time he has been here," Tom Gray replied, but then thought again. "No, not at first. When he came here first he had no car and he needed one so he bought an old car, one of these ones with the wood round about them on the outside. I have never owned a car so I don't what kind that was. They were common enough at one time."

"What colour was it Mr Gray?"

"Dark green. It was a good looking car but Jones said it would do 'til he got a better one. He worked for a while and he must have got enough to change to that silver car and has had it ever since."

"He looks after it though." Fleming commented.

"He spent a lot of time on it," Tom agreed, "especially the inside. I walked past it one day and the smell of bleach would have knocked you out. I think he overdid it at times but as you say, Mr Fleming, it was clean."

"He never had a garage?"

"I dare say he would have liked one but he would have had to build it himself, or at his own expense. He wouldn't go to that bother." Tom believed.

"Did he ever have friends or relatives visiting him?"

"No. I don't think he had any." Tom said in a slightly sympathetic tone. "I once got a letter through my letter box meant for him. He wasn't long here and the postie still didn't know his name. It was addressed to somebody 'John' instead of 'Jones'. I stuck it through his letter box."

"That was the right thing to do, Tom." Fleming said with a smile.

"Listen Tom, I better be going but I will look by when I get back on dayshift. In the meantime keep your doors and windows tight, okay? I'll let the CID know that your sledgehammer is missing."

"Thanks Andy, that was good of you to come by and to get me these fags."

SEVEN

Detective Chief Inspector Raymond Adam was feeling positive and happy, like a child on Christmas morning. He was receiving good responses and every unopened envelope was opened with optimism. The laboratory had confirmed that the blood spatter on the roughcast wall at 24 Heather Road had indeed been consistent with the blood of Morton Grant. The ballpeen hammer had been coated in identical blood and brain matter, again consistent with the victim. Enquiries conducted by CID officers in Manchester and West Midlands had shown that Bert Jones had qualified as documented at Manchester University, on a course where the first year had included a field study in Scotland. He had worked as a mortuary assistant in a private hospital where the cadavers had been exclusively children.

These results were not giving him the name of a murderer, but they were fitting out a suspect in murderer's clothing. Adam felt he had every reason to believe that Bert Jones was the right guy for the murder of Morton Grant.

Raymond Adam knew that Corran Bay was not a place

THE TALE OF THE OLD SCHOOL TIES

to provide child killers and had a history of raising very few killers of any kind. He had promised to keep his colleagues in Kent and Surrey informed and he lifted the telephone with the pleasure of one who has glad tidings.

On his way back from Tom Gray's house, Fleming looked in at the office to see Campbell but the CID were out. He looked at the telex messages and reports in Dougie Campbell's 'in' tray and saw that Sally Armstrong had reported her enquiry at the former paediatric hospital. He then left to join Mary for coffee.

At home that evening, Andrew Fleming waited until the children were in bed and Mary was watching a favourite television programme before making his phone call. He held in his hand the card given to him by 'Dick', his friend in military intelligence. After a series of clicks and bleeps Fleming got through.

"Dick, this is Andy Fleming. I wonder if you can help with this child abduction business."

"Give me your number, the one you are on right now and I will call you straight back."

This procedure followed, Fleming lifted his phone.

"Keep it brief, Andy, but give me all I need." Dick said tersely.

"Letherford School. What connection does the surname 'Johns' have to the school, in terms of past pupils, teachers, masters, trustees, applicants or parents?"

"I will call you back on this number at the same time

tomorrow. If there is a positive answer you will have it. By the way Freddie sends his regards. Keep safe old boy, Goodbye." With that the line went dead. Fleming smiled.

James Barrowman was delighted to hear of the positive aspects of the circumstantial evidence pointing to this bloke Jones. The car belonging to Jones, of which he had been informed at an early stage, had actually shown up on some of the CCTV footage and seemed to place this man Jones in the area of Letherford School at the material time. The film in most of CCTV footage was hazy and could never positively identify Jones as the driver and none of the pictures of his car showed a child passenger. The real strength of this evidence lay in the distance between the home address of Jones and the area he had travelled to at the time of the abduction. Simply put, why was he in Kent at all? The Detective had spoken to John Wetherby about his 'profiling' theory and had asked Wetherby if the name Jones meant anything in terms of past staff or pupils. There had been several pupils and parents of the name Jones but none called Bert Jones. The two Robert Jones' had been traced. They resided in the south of England with no knowledge of the suspect individual and both had substantiated alibis for the times of the abductions.

The Crime Prevention sergeant who had attended at the hospital to interview Valetta Johns had circulated a

THE TALE OF THE OLD SCHOOL TIES

lookout for her son, Harvey Johns. Due to the nature of the known crime, malicious damage to a headstone, circulation was confined to the local force areas. In order to do this the sergeant had submitted a report on the damage, contrary to the original wishes of Mrs Johns and had spoken to Graeme Benson to confirm the details of the deceased and the singular and seemingly personal motive for this offence.

He had already enquired as to previous convictions for Harvey Johns but there were none on record.

The complaints made by the girls at Mary Upton School had led to press coverage and dismissal for Harvey Johns but not to criminal convictions. These schools could be guarded and publicity conscious to a fault. As John Wetherby knew, reputation was everything.

Raymond Adam was experiencing the impact of the same difficulty. Perfectly clear fingerprints had been recovered from the handle of the ballpeen hammer but they failed to match any record at the Criminal Records Office. From this point, matters just got worse.

He had hoped and expected that the 'napkin rings' recovered from Jones' kitchen waste bin would be identified as the sawn up plaster cast being worn by Helen Holloway on the day she had gone missing from the Mary Upton School in Surrey the previous year. He was disappointed to hear that the 'rings' had come from a large animal bone, too large to have been human. The bone had been bleached white by age. When the rings had been placed side by side in their original position, the outer surface had not been signed by school friends, merely marked with a reference number in black marker pen. Raymond Adam had called Mark Goodfellow but the bone had not come from the marine lab.

It was clear to the Detective Chief Inspector that his case against Bert Jones for the murder of Morton Grant was strong, despite the lack of obvious motive. The link with the abductions in Kent and Surrey had been shown to be possible but had not been established. Where did Jones get that animal bone?

Fleming had heard that Professor Halbooth had returned home and he decided to look in as he was passing, to meet the professor and, as a matter of propriety, inform him of the missing person enquiry in respect of Anthony, together with its successful conclusion. As Anthony was still a minor in terms of such things, it was the right thing to do.

The professor was very interested in the sequence of events related by Andrew Fleming, not through any anxiety for Anthony, but the administrative considerations around the tracing of persons reported missing. It was an interest with the human element extracted.

"I probably felt less concerned about Anthony than I should have been, Professor Halbooth. He is a very intelligent boy and quite adequately equipped to find his way around but he is still a young man and not able to roam without intimating his intentions."

"Yes. If that is the letter of the law then it has to be respected." the professor said, missing the point and virtually confirming his own lack of concern over his wandering son.

Fleming had again been drawn to the photograph of the family group beside the Morris Traveller but said nothing. He had previously noted the registration number and he was again reminded to check it out. It was something that old Tom Gray had spoken about.

Anthony had sat quietly in the background while his father and Fleming had been in conversation but now he spoke out.

"Mrs Campbell asked me to remind you, Constable Fleming, that Morton Grant had library books to return."

"Right Anthony, I'll see what I can do about that."

That evening Fleming received his promised telephone call from his friend 'Dick'.

"I am sorry, Andrew. I think I may have what you are after but the facts of the matter are so sensitive that we should not discuss them on the telephone. Not everything can be described as 'public record'. I shall be coming over shortly and I will ask for you to attend personally. We can discuss this matter then. Sorry for the delay but I think you can understand."

"I trust you to be right, Dick. I am not a patient type

but this time I suppose I have to be. Thanks for calling back. Look forward to seeing you."

When he began nightshift that night Fleming did check the Police National Computer for the current owner of the old Morris Traveller and found that it was registered to a man in Dumfries. After calling directory enquiries he had a telephone number for the owner but the hour was not really appropriate to be making the phone call.

In the meantime he took to the street and gradually made his way to the public house that had been used regularly on Friday and Saturday nights by Morton Grant. He asked among the regulars as to who had been in contact with Morton on his last night as a customer. Two men who worked with a different department of the council said that they had spoken to him and drank with him until he left at his customary eleven o'clock, just as the bartender had previously told Fleming.

These men told Fleming that Morton had been in good spirits and his talk had been along the usual imaginary but entertaining lines. He had expected to carry out a mission for the mafia. They had 'fingered' a hit man for Morton to deal with. The council painter knew where to find his man but the whole business was 'hush-hush'. At any other time Fleming would have been as amused and laughing, just as the witnesses had been at the time, but nobody was laughing now.

"You boys work with the Cleansing Department, don't

you? Do many people put their rubbish into black bags before they put it in their bins?"

"Aye, quite a few do that, but then you have places like the hospital and the marine lab that do it all the time." one of the men answered. His mate nodded in agreement.

"Everything from there is in a black bag?" Fleming asked.

"That's right, some sort of health rule. Biological waste is different again. It is in yellow bags and goes for incineration."

"It never gets opened?" Fleming asked.

"Who would want to open that lot?"

Sophie Rinstead looked out through the slats of her lounge window down to the car park below. She was concerned to see the silver car sitting in one of the parking spaces designated to residents of the flats. The same silver car with the same male driver had followed her from the school where she worked to the supermarket and then from the supermarket to her home the previous evening. Now this guy was back again. Sophie knew that the man was not someone from the flats and she had never seen his car before yesterday. At this distance she could not make out the car number but she thought it might be worthwhile to go down and take a note of it. There was something threatening about this man. She actually took her small camera and walked out into the car park where she purposefully stood opposite the car and took a photograph before hurrying back into the building, behind the safety of the security doors. The car left immediately.

Sophie intended to go into Leamington that day to look at some clothing and meet a friend for coffee. This was still her intention but the driver of the silver car had unnerved her. She called her father and told him about her worrying experience.

He assured her that she would be all right during daylight hours and in busy shopping centres. If the man showed up again she could report him to the police as a stalker but she would need the car number, something she had only photographed, and an idea of what he looked like.

She collected her things and put her camera into her handbag. As she closed the flat door and put her keys into her handbag, she realised that she was doing everything in a rush. Instinctively she wanted out of the building and into her car before the silver car appeared again.

Sophie was glad to reach Leamington town centre without seeing anyone who could be the stalker. She parked in a back street and walked through to the shops. The broad pavements allowed her to see everyone in both directions. Once inside the clothes shops she felt reasonably safe from anyone in a silver car.

At 3 p.m. she went to the small coffee shop that she and Trish always used and was happy to find her friend waiting for her.

As they sat over large cappuccinos, the friends discussed

clothes, school, teaching and make-up. Sophie told Trish about the strange man in the silver car. They joked about her brave act of photography and Sophie found that she was making light of the matter, sounding less concerned than she really was.

"You just can't be careful enough these days," Trish told her. "Did you hear about Mrs Templeton?"

Sophie Rinstead looked alarmed.

"No. What happened to her?"

"It was just recently. She answered her door to be knocked down and beaten unconscious by some man she didn't know. A month ago that could have been Lorna."

"Does Lorna know?" Sophie wondered. "How is her mum?"

"She is going to be all right, apparently. That was just the night before last, but Lorna has spoken to her mum on the phone."

"Did this man steal anything?" Sophie asked.

"No, but he did go through the house, so he had a good look but never took anything."

"I must go to see her." Sophie said, shaking her head in disbelief. "Have you been in, to the hospital I mean?"

"Yes," Trish replied. "I was there yesterday but I could go back in with you if you want."

That Saturday afternoon Fleming telephoned the Dumfries number and spoke to William Menzies, the man who currently owned the old Morris Traveller in the

Halbooth's family photograph. After explaining who he was, Fleming went on to assure Mr Menzies that there was no problem regarding his purchase or ownership of the car.

"What I need to know, Mr Menzies, is precisely when did you buy the car and from whom?"

"I can tell you that Constable, just give me a second to look out my files. I have a small collection of Morris cars. I keep them in good order and my files are just as good."

He spent a few moments away from the phone looking into his files and then came back on.

"I bought that car on Saturday 12th July 1980 from a man called Bert Jones. He came from up your way, I believe, 24 Heather Road. I always get a receipt, you see. The car was immaculately clean, I remember that. He was going to buy a Ford or so he told me. I gave him a run into Dumfries from here and that was the last that I saw of him."

"Did he tell you how long he had owned the car?" Fleming asked.

"Not exactly, but I got the impression he had not owned it all that long. He complained about the consumption he was getting with it. He expected better. I suppose with the price of petrol now who could blame him? It is not a problem for me because I am not running the cars too much."

"Have you been cleaning it much?" Fleming asked, hoping to prompt some 'guess what I found' response.

THE TALE OF THE OLD SCHOOL TIES

"Every bit as much as he did." Menzies replied.

"Good for you." Fleming said with more admiration than he was feeling.

When Sophie and Trish entered the ward Sophie was aghast at the sight of Mrs Templeton. Her bruising and swelling made her barely recognisable. A red abrasion ran round her neck like a necklace.

"It's all right Sophie. It looks worse than it feels now, my dear. At least Lorna is not here to see me and she won't see me when she phones."

"That is just as well, Mrs Templeton. She would probably feel guilty about this. She is only gone a month." Sophie said, taking the old lady's hand and kissing it. To kiss her on the cheek might have been painful for Mrs Templeton.

"Yes. I am missing her so much, but don't tell her that. If you are writing or phoning just tell her I am fine and managing well. She has her own life to lead and you are only young once as they say."

"You stay in a good area Mrs Templeton. I would have expected you to be safe from an attack like this. What was that man doing there?" Sophie asked, still holding the older lady's hand.

"That is a real mystery, Sophie. He actually looked surprised to see me when I opened the door but he never ran away. He just pushed me in and battered me about the head and then put a rope round my neck and started to pull on it. He asked me where Lorna was. I might have told him 'Australia' but I was gasping for breath so I don't know if he would hear me. I blacked out and I knew nothing until the ambulance men got me round."

"Who had called for the ambulance?" Trish asked.

"That's what the police wanted to know," Mrs Templeton said. "The ambulance people had called the police but who called for the ambulance. The police reckon it had to be the man that attacked me. Why would he do that?"

Sophie offered no explanation but wondered if Mrs Templeton had really been the attackers intended victim.

"He asked for Lorna and he went through the house after attacking you?" Sophie asked in order to be sure of her facts.

"Yes dear. Do you suppose he had come to the wrong house?"

James Barrowman was an extremely frustrated man. A month had now passed since the abduction of William Johnston Faraday and he was no further forward. He had heard from Raymond Adam that a search of Jones' house had failed to produce evidence connecting Jones' to the child abductions as Adam had hoped. The extensive searching of film footage had not provided better photographs of Jones' or his car. He was aware that Surrey were not making progress but then that was their problem and would have no subduing effect on the anger of the Faraday parents.

THE TALE OF THE OLD SCHOOL TIES

The boy's blood-stained clothing, which did not include his school tie, had provided grey fibres consistent with the carpets of a Ford car. Barrowman had requested enquiry from all forces with independent schools in their areas to provide details of any complaints or reports from these schools of incidents involving persons or vehicles prowling on school grounds, making approaches to pupils and any incident suggesting that the culprit of Letherford and Mary Upton Schools' abductions might have been active elsewhere.

Responses so far had not been promising. If they continued to be negative then the pattern would be as limited as it had first appeared.

At Letherford School the headmaster was in a similar despondency. John Wetherby had remained in attendance each day, hoping for news of William Faraday, but more realistically protecting his own position. That Saturday afternoon marked one month since the boy's disappearance and it was acknowledged by a visit from Lord Brackston.

There was nothing much to report but Wetherby felt vindicated by the chairman's impromptu appearance. The men discussed the situation in the way that professional men do, psychologically suggesting that they were somehow contributing in some way. They soon ran out of constructive observations and turned to more general conversation.

"I had a visit a couple of weeks back from a young lad

from Scotland," Wetherby said in the hope of being amusing. "He wanted to know why his father had not been given the science master's post in school ten years ago."

"Yes, you told me. What was his name, the father I mean?"

"Eh Halbooth, I believe. I do not recall the first name." Wetherby replied.

"Oh yes, Milton Halbooth, clever chap, he is a professor in pharmaceuticals. What did you tell the boy?"

"I told him that the position had been filled by the only applicant with previous teaching experience." Wetherby said. "I had no way of knowing who the applicants had been other than our current science master."

Lord Brackston laughed.

"Well done, old fellow, very shrewd, not strictly true but very shrewd."

"There was a teacher applicant?" Wetherby asked.

"There was. He may not have appeared on any forms you have for the same reasons that he was not considered. A chap called Johns, but he had a damn cheek even applying. He had been at Mary Upton."

"Was he not worth considering?" Wetherby asked.

"Not with that man's pedigree." Lord Brackston answered abruptly. "Now you really must start spending time at home, John. Your attitude during this testing time has been admirable but you have a life and family of your own. The next school year will not be kinder to you for the conscientiousness you have shown. Your family deserve your attention too. Nobody will think less of you. You are on holiday old chap. Give that Barrowman fellow your home number if it makes you feel better but show your face at home."

It was with the utmost trepidation that Sophie Rinstead returned to her flat that evening. She sat in her locked car until she saw Todd Russell coming home. Todd was a burly chap who lived on the floor above her and worked lateshift with an engineering firm. She explained to Todd that a man had followed her home the night before and asked to accompany him until she could safely enter her own flat.

"No problem Sophie. I'm going your way anyway." he joked.

As they walked in and climbed the stairs Sophie explained the silver car and told Todd of how she had taken a photograph of it.

"No paranoia then." he joked again. "Here we are Sophie, now open up and go in."

"No, wait Todd, can you come in with me?"

"You really are scared, aren't you?" he said without the smile. "Of course, Sophie, I'll be here. In you go."

He accompanied her to each room, checking cupboards and wardrobes. As they came back into the lounge Todd Russell was in front of Sophie and found a man standing in the entrance doorway holding a short length of rope. As soon as he saw Todd this man took off running down the stairs. Sophie screamed and Todd Russell chased after the smaller man. The difference in stature seemed to favour the intruder on the tight twisting staircase. A few minutes later and a sweating, gasping Todd Russell returned to the door of the flat.

"Sorry, Sophie, he got away. He had a silver car parked round the corner just like you said, but he drove away without lights. I never saw the number. Best to call the police. I'll leave you my phone number, you can call me anytime that I'm home to see you out or coming in. In the meantime call the cops."

The Sunday afternoon sunshine beat down on Fleming as he walked with Mary and the children along the sandy beach just two minutes away from their home. The far end of the beach was busy with holiday-makers from a camp site but the closer end was quiet and that was where locals met other locals in the course of walking. As the Flemings headed back they met the Hardistys.

"I can't believe that you don't have a camera round your neck Duncan." Fleming said, greeting his neighbour.

"My day off, remember?" Duncan said with a broad smile. "But I'll have it tomorrow morning from four o'clock, I'm heading for the War Memorial at Spean Bridge, want to come?"

"I'll still be working, Duncan. Tonight's my last nightshift."

THE TALE OF THE OLD SCHOOL TIES

Mary was separately engaged in conversation with Rebecca Hardisty over their children and the difference it made to have them at home during the week. The children themselves had gone off to the water's edge to throw stones or shells into the sea.

"Remember you once told me about a Morris Traveller you caught in a shot at Loch Leven?" Andy Fleming asked Duncan.

"Yes, I remember. What about it?"

"Would you happen to know the date of that shot?" Fleming asked.

"I still have the photograph somewhere, Andy. The time and the date will be on the back of it. Do you want it?"

"That would depend on what the picture shows, Duncan, front and back. I won't know until I have seen it."

"I'll look it out for you, Andy and bring it round. If it's late, I'll drop it through your letter box."

"Thanks, Duncan."

Mary Ainsworth was visiting Mrs Johns that afternoon and found her more cheerful. There was a return of colour to the old lady's complexion and the staff had been talking of her going home shortly.

"That is good, Mrs Johns. You must be sure to let me know and I'll be there to meet you." Mary said.

"I do not think it will be before Tuesday at the earliest,

Mary. I have agreed with the sergeant to wait until my house has some security improvements." Mrs Johns said with a smile. "I have promised to pay for them."

"Sounds like a good idea." Mary agreed. "I do not want you coming back in here again."

"I do not wish for either of us to be in here." Valetta said with a suggestion of consideration for Mary. "Mind you the girls in this ward have been very good, but a hospital is still a hospital, better off at home."

"When are these people coming to install the security, Mrs Johns?"

"Tomorrow morning at eight-thirty, Mary, could you be there to let them in? The sergeant will be looking by to ensure that the proper equipment is to hand and that the job is going ahead as planned."

The Sunday nightshift was relatively quiet, particularly after 2 a.m. and Fleming spent time walking from Morton's favourite pub to 24 Heather Road. He tried to emulate Morton's walk, a recognisable gait which had formed part of his character and never varied in pace whether drunk or sober.

The walk took twenty minutes. That was too short. Mr Gray had spoken of being disturbed around midnight. Would Morton have gone home first and then walked to Heather Road? He might have wanted a torch and perhaps a bag to take away whatever he found. Probably. Fleming did the same walk in reverse, only this time went

THE TALE OF THE OLD SCHOOL TIES

via Morton Grant's council house, allowing five minutes at home for the big man to find what he wanted plus the toilet. While waiting at Morton's house Fleming decided to look in his dustbin. The bin should have been emptied mid-week but nobody had thought to put it out for collection. On top of other household rubbish was a page or two of newspaper holding a white cardboard tray. Morton had evidently stopped for a fish supper to eat as he walked home.

This time the walk took 50 minutes and allowing for time spent at the chip shop Morton had spent an hour in reaching Heather Road, coinciding comfortably with Tom Gray's story of being disturbed around midnight.

Fleming looked again at the note he had been handed by Morton on the day he had died. 'Black parcel man 24 Heather Road' was what it said. Surely Morton would not have written this note, put it in an envelope and broken with his conventional behaviour by handing it to Fleming personally, on the strength of seeing Jones place a black bag in his dustbin? He had to have seen more to inspire his 'tip' to Fleming and then followed it up with a lengthy walk to Heather Road in order to search Jones' dustbin. His own curiosity had seen him killed, poor soul, but what had caused such great curiosity? What had there been at 24 Heather Road to find that could not be found now?

On Monday morning two vans with the livery of a national security firm arrived outside Mrs Johns' home to be met by Mary Ainsworth. The security workmen began to unload ladders and boxed equipment from their vehicles and Mary unlocked the house to give them access. Five minutes later the police sergeant appeared on the scene and spoke with one of the men, occasionally pointing out windows and doors as he spoke, before accompanying the men into the house.

From the kerb fifty yards down the street a silver car moved out and drove away.

Mary Ainsworth felt relaxed with four men working in and around the place but her mind kept thinking of her earlier visit to the house with the sergeant. Someone had been in the house the night before and now it would seem to have been Mrs Johns' estranged son. Had he pushed his own mother down the stairs? She had been at pains to ignore the matter and she had not described a situation in which her son had been present. Even if she had fallen by accident with him there, had he callously left the house with his mother lying unresponsive at the foot of the stairs?

Celia Kirkwood had washed all her brother Morton's bedding for the last time and was folding it neatly into cardboard boxes given to her by her friend at the shoe shop. Council worker or not, murder victim or not, Morton Grant's tenancy had come to an end and the council only permitted so long before the house should be rendered vacant. Celia had not helped matters. She had

THE TALE OF THE OLD SCHOOL TIES

been unwilling to enter the house until today. Her brother had been dead for only a week but she still felt the shock of his early and unexpected death. Celia would manage to clear the house by the council deadline but she still felt the sad reluctance of being there.

She had complained to Morton so often about his washing, surely he could do it himself, she had her own home to think of. Now she was seeing her brother's clothes for the last time. She had set aside his best suit with a shirt and tie. The funeral had not yet been arranged, something to do with it 'being a Fiscal death', the undertaker had said.

There was a gentle tap on the house door and Celia turned to see a man looking in round the edge of the door. She recognised the face but couldn't place him.

"Can I help you?" she asked.

"I am Andrew Fleming, a local police officer. I think you are Celia, Morton's sister, is that right?"

"Yes, I am Celia Kirkwood, originally Celia Grant. I am just clearing up his things." she said as if her presence required explanation. She now recognised Fleming despite the absence of uniform.

"Did you know this house well, Celia? Were you here much?" Fleming asked.

"Yes," she said as if her reply amounted to a massive understatement. "I hate to think what this house would have been like without my visits."

Fleming smiled at this.

"Was Morton really that untidy?" Fleming asked as if he could not believe it.

"With paint he was neat and tidy, with everything else, no. Why are you interested?" Celia asked.

"I knew Morton. I had the same soft spot for him as everyone else. I have been trying to figure out what reason anyone could have to murder him." Fleming said seriously. "I just wondered if Morton had something here at home to offer an indication of that. I know he was suspicious of something. I just need to find out what it was."

"Like I say, Mr Fleming, Morton was never the most tidy of men but he did keep a notebook and pamphlets in his overalls. I have thrown the pamphlets out but I kept the notebook. It is in that box there."

She indicated a smaller box which held watches, pens, electric razor, sunglasses, coins, cuff links and two small hardback notebooks. Fleming lifted the first of these books and recognised Morton's handwriting from the note on the envelope. The book held sequential entries, each under the heading of the working date. Beneath the date there were lists of jobs done, giving details of hours worked and paint used. The location was always given and recalling what Tom Gray had told him, Fleming looked back to the week before Morton's death. He found where Morton had recorded his painting of lamp standards in Heather Road. He had noted a car registration number in his entry. It was Bert Jones' car number. There was nothing else in that day's entry other than details of his work. Fleming lifted a second book. In this he found more random entries separated by underlining in the same manner as his work book.

Beneath the same date heading was an entry that said, '24 Heather Road – guy decides not to use dustbin for black plastic bag when he sees me watching – will attend later.'

"Did Morton have any torches here, Celia?" Fleming asked.

"Yes, he had a big wide one that Mike and I gave him at Christmas. It was in here." she said, crossing to the kitchen and a cupboard near to the back door. "Oh, it's not there."

"What did it look like?" Fleming asked. "It might turn up somewhere."

Celia described the powerful torch of black plastic construction that was missing from a cupboard where tools and brushes were stored in a neat arrangement with everything else in its normal place.

"Do you mind if I hold on to these books of Morton's in the meantime, Celia? I think they might be useful. You'll get them back, of course."

"By all means, Mr Fleming, they were probably destined for the dustbin anyway."

"On the subject of books, Celia, Morton had library books..."

Sophie Rinstead had called the police following the intrusion of the stranger. She and Todd Russell had given statements to the police but she had been encouraged to have her photographic film developed so that the registration mark of the silver car could become known. She had done that, using a 24 hour return service and went directly to the police station with the photograph. The police officer who had asked her for the results of her photograph was not on duty but the man she spoke to said he would leave it for Constable Crane, the officer who was dealing with the incident.

Thomas Crane was on duty a few hours later and took the photograph to the control room, requesting a PNC check on the owner of the car shown. He was given the photograph back with a note showing 'Bert Jones, 24 Heather Road, Corran Bay, Argyll – speak to CID regarding this car and owner'.

Constable Crane took his photograph and note to the CID and asked what significance his prowler had. After some searching through past telex circulations, the Detective Inspector informed him that there was a lookout for this car and its owner in respect of a murder in Scotland. When Thomas Crane had explained in detail the incident he had attended at Sophie's flat the Detective Inspector decided to update the earlier circulation to show that the car and its owner were now in his area and the wanted man was active and posed a threat. His circulation was read by James Barrowman, Raymond Adam and Dennis Howell, the Surrey Detective Chief Inspector recently assigned to the Helen Holloway case. The case had been resuscitated by the forensic report showing that fibres from a bone in a black plastic bag in a Scottish highland peat bog were identical to the fibres of a Mary Upton school uniform.

On Tuesday 27th July, Mrs Valetta Johns was allowed home from hospital. It had been one week since she had been found at the bottom of her own stairs. Mary was there to meet her and see her settled into her armchair. The nurse who had accompanied Mrs Johns in the ambulance left Mary in charge of Mrs Johns' medication, explaining its purpose and use to both ladies.

Once alone together, Mary made tea for Valetta who seemed excited to be home. Mary began to tell her of the security gadgets installed around the house and switched on the television to show Mrs Johns how, on a given channel selection, she could see four camera views of the front and back of her house and four internal views at any time she chose. When the television was showing any other channel or was switched off, the camera views were still being recorded with the time and date and could be viewed retrospectively. A security alarm system had also been installed to deter any would-be burglar.

The old lady was delighted with her new 'toys' and told Mary that she felt happier about her home now.

"I think it should be obvious to anyone outside that this house is protected now." she told Mary Ainsworth. "Even Harvey should know better than to come in here."

Mary had been asked by the police sergeant about this son called Harvey, but Mary had to say that she had never known of his existence until last week's incident.

"What is wrong with your son, dear, that he would want to harm you or to damage your husband's headstone?"

Mrs Johns stopped smiling and looked down at the carpet, considering whether to inform Mary or not. It would be true to say that Mary was in her home enough to be under a certain risk from Harvey.

"He is dangerous, Mary. Ever since he was a child he has had a fascination with death. He had no brothers or sisters and we bought him a puppy dog. For a few weeks he played with the little thing but then we found it dead beneath the hedge. He had chopped off its head, so we knew that it had not been an accident. He denied it but Wesley gave him a hell of a row. There would be no more pets for Harvey. We buried the poor little dog and never told anyone the truth about how it had died. He was clever at school but he had no close friends, not friends that wanted to come to his house to play or to have him come to theirs. We could tell that his sadistic streak was still there. He must have trapped birds in the garden and we would find them methodically dissected, hardly the work of a cat."

"That sounds terrible." said Mary. "Could you not have him helped?"

"Wesley wouldn't hear of it. Of course, my husband

THE TALE OF THE OLD SCHOOL TIES

was thinking of himself and his personal reputation. He began to treat Harvey as though he was already a disappointment. The boy could not stand the put-down and reacted noisily to his father's insults or comments. As he became older, Harvey was more vicious and once or twice hit out at Wesley. My husband was an old man and not fit to take the physical violence. He refused to let other people know that his son was given to such moods and attacks. He just kept out of his way."

"That would be safer for your husband." Mary suggested.

"Yes, it was and Wesley cut back on the insults to the point where he simply ignored the boy. Harvey went off to university and graduated in chemistry and biology, always his strong subjects. His father never went to his graduation, I went on my own."

"You were right to go." Mary suggested, expecting to be supportive.

"No, apparently not, Mary, Harvey resented my presence. He said I was only there to emphasise his father's hatred towards him. He had been rejected, why wouldn't I just admit it?"

"That was cruel." Mary ventured.

"I thought so, Mary. I left in tears."

"But he started teaching," Mary remarked. "And he got himself married."

"That's true but only when the ties had been severed. We learned about his teaching position only after he had secured alternative accommodation for himself. His marriage to Cynthia Ascot was something that happened very quickly and actually took Wesley and me by surprise. We learned about that from the newspaper."

"Oh dear, how awful for you," Mary sympathised.

"Cynthia thought so too. She phoned me, actually she phoned me several times, because she had wanted to know Harvey's parents. The last of her phone calls were different, the girl was afraid. Harvey had been dismissed from his school position as a result of complaints made against him."

"That would be what that girl, Sophie, was talking about." Mary said.

"And she was lying," Mrs Johns said angrily. "Harvey would take that as a rejection and Cynthia would be to blame. However, Harvey has been an accident waiting to happen as far as I am concerned. He is just so fractious and unpredictable. Cynthia had come to realise that I suspect, and as for her suicide," Valetta Johns did not finish but stared into space, temporarily spellbound by her own thought.

"Another puppy dog, perhaps?" Mary suggested.

Valetta Johns seemed not to have heard her.

"You know, he actually applied for a position at Letherford after he had been dismissed from Mary Upton?" Mrs Johns said as if talking to herself. "What did he expect to happen? He was rejected again, of course."

She returned from her reverie and turned to face Mary.

"Yes, Mary. I wouldn't be surprised if Cynthia became another puppy dog."

"What about you, Mrs Johns? Do you suppose that Harvey knew you were alive when he left? He never stopped to offer you help, I cannot forgive that." Mary said a little heatedly.

"I don't hate him, Mary. That's not what mothers do."

That afternoon Fleming began his late-shift week and spoke to Douglas Campbell about the progress of the murder enquiry into the death of Morton Grant. He learned about the circulation regarding the foiled attack on the girl in Warwickshire. Jones was in England and still at large with this silver Ford.

"What did you find when you searched his flat?" Fleming asked.

"Not a lot as it happens," Campbell said. "I thought we had recovered a plaster cast that would have come from the missing girl but it turned out to be a hollow bone, an animal bone with a number written on it."

He looked at Fleming expecting him to laugh but Fleming wasn't laughing.

"The guy had a tray of tools," Campbell continued. "Including a hacksaw that we took, but it had been used to cut the bone, not plaster. The place was spotless, Andy. I've never seen a house so clean when there was only one bloke staying there."

"Any clothes?" Fleming asked.

"Yeah, there were clothes, suits, shirts, ties, socks, T-shirts, pants, the lot. He left in a hurry, remember?"

"So who has the blood-stained clothes, Dougie?"

"He probably tossed them." Campbell replied glibly.

"I suppose he had black bin bags?" Fleming asked.

Campbell nodded.

At that point Raymond Adam arrived and Fleming left the CID men to get back to his own work. He was driving past the library when he thought he saw young Anthony Halbooth walking in. He turned and went back to the library car park. When Anthony came out Fleming beckoned him over.

"More Roman wisdom, Anthony?"

The boy smiled.

"With a little help from the Greeks," the boy replied.

"Anthony, you know that old green Morris Traveller that your dad owned? When did he sell it?" Fleming asked.

Anthony looked defensive but then realised that Fleming was not sounding more than interested.

"That was in 1980, probably about April or May," he remembered. "Mother had been using the car to commute weekly to the Natural History museum. She was working on the return of exhibits after the extension was completed. When she finished with that father sold the car."

"Do you recall who bought it?" Fleming asked without suggestion.

"All I can remember was father saying that he had sold

it to a fellow scientist. He seemed to be pleased about that, don't ask me why."

"Would your father have cleaned out the car before selling it?" Fleming asked with a smile.

Anthony laughed out loud. Fleming had not expected to hear the boy laugh at any time.

"Father clean out his car? He would not know where to begin and would fail to understand the point of doing it. Why do you think we have Gretchen? But she wouldn't clean out the car either. The answer is definitely 'no'."

"That is what I thought." Fleming said.

"Mrs Campbell says she has the books back from that poor man's house." Anthony said, confirming that his message to Fleming concerning the return of Morton Grant's books had been attended to by Celia, someone Mrs Campbell had known without being aware of her connection to Morton.

"Aye, poor Morton, he won't be coming here for more books now." Fleming said. "Is your dad still home, Anthony?"

"I think so." Anthony answered, making Fleming laugh at his uncertainty.

"Then come with me. I want to go and see him."

"What did Fleming have to say about the Morton Grant murder?" Raymond Adam asked Douglas Campbell.

"He was suggesting that the blood-stained clothing

would not be among the clothes at the flat." Campbell said with sarcasm.

"I doubt that he has spent the last week thinking about that." Adam replied. He knew Fleming and would always expect him to know more than he was prepared to say.

When the police vehicle reached the lodge house Anthony led Fleming into the house and they found Professor Halbooth holding up a glass covered frame of dead moths.

"Oh hello, Officer Fleming. This was my father's. I think we should put it out. What do you think, Anthony?"

"I've always thought that we should put it out, father." Anthony said flatly.

"Then we shall." the professor said firmly, as he placed the frame back on its picture hook.

"Constable Fleming has some questions to ask you, father, about your old Morris car." Anthony said by way of placing Fleming and the professor on the same page.

"Oh, I have sold it, I'm afraid," the professor said politely.

"Yes sir, I know, but when and to whom?"

"Oh now, I should have that information in this file," the professor said, crossing to a shelf with box files. He took down a box file with the word 'cars' in block capitals down the label. He opened the file and rummaged among the trapped papers until he eventually came to a receipt.

"Here we are. Ah, that's where I have heard the name

Bert Jones before. He is the marine lab man who bought my car after your mother brought it back from the museum."

Anthony chuckled at the way his father had suggested an even greater vintage for the Morris. Fleming smiled but not for long.

"What was the date of the sale, Professor Halbooth?"

The professor showed Fleming the document.

"Wednesday, 4th of June, 1980." he replied, pointing to the date written at the top of the page.

"Had anyone cleaned out the car?" Fleming asked, trying hard not to smile.

"Not in fifteen years." the professor replied, puzzled by the laughter of the other two.

EIGHT

Detective Chief Inspector Raymond Adam drove across the narrow bridge and took his car as far onto the grass verge as he dared. He parked there and walked back to the point where it was reasonable to assume that Morton Grant had been dropped onto the side of the railway line. As he surveyed the area beneath he could scarcely believe what he was seeing. Andrew Fleming was walking among the bracken and grass on the slope to his left. As he looked to his right the DCI saw Constable Hamish MacLeod searching the slope on the opposite side of the track. There was no sign of a police vehicle and these officers had clearly walked to this spot, probably along the railway line.

"What are you looking for?" he called out to Fleming who was closer.

"Anything that's here." was the reply.

Adam muttered his expletives but accepted that these two were probably doing something that should have been done by now. On his way back to his car there were more obscenities to the effect that Fleming might try to solve this murder without him. He would go back to the

THE TALE OF THE OLD SCHOOL TIES

station and wait for him. That would be easier than climbing down steep slopes onto a railway line.

"Well, did you find anything?" he asked as soon as Fleming and MacLeod returned to the office.

"I'm afraid not, sir." Fleming said with a sigh. "But we looked."

Raymond Adam ignored the implied criticism.

"What do you know about this murder, Andy? I could use some inspiration here."

"You could use some help, I agree, sir," Fleming said. "I am pretty much stuck in the theory side of this myself at the moment but I expect to have answers in the next few days. If my theories go up in smoke you won't need to know but if I am right I will be sure to give you what I learn immediately."

"You want my home number?" Adam asked as he saw Fleming begin to move away.

"I've got it, sir." Fleming replied without turning round.

"You're an insubordinate git, Fleming." Adam remarked to the constable's back.

"Aye, I'm a resourceful insubordinate git, sir." Fleming said without stopping or turning.

Adam smiled to himself and muttered, "Fair enough."

Fleming finished work at eleven and drove straight home. He was pleased to see that his lounge light was on, Mary must be up watching television.

When he went into his house he found Duncan Hardisty sitting in the lounge talking to Mary.

"Caught you pair at last." Fleming joked. "How are you doing Duncan?"

"Duncan is up waiting for you, Andy," Mary explained. "Do you want coffee?"

"No dear, just two glasses."

"Oh, I see. Well, I am off to bed, good night Duncan."

With two glasses of Ledaig single malt, the men were ready to look at the photograph Duncan had brought. It was an 8 by 10 shot with a dry dirt lay-by in the foreground and a sunlit metal bridge in the background. Parked in the lay-by was a dark green Morris 1000 Traveller similar to that once owned by Professor Halbooth. The view of the car was oblique but the registration number did appear to be identical to the very same car. Between the car and the water there was the figure of a man who was apparently walking towards the water's edge.

"Have you any idea who this guy is, Duncan?"

"He was the car driver and he was carrying something in his hands," said Duncan, shrugging his shoulders. "Whatever it was, he wasn't carrying it when he came back to his car and drove away."

"Did he just throw something into the water?" Andy asked.

"No, he spent time putting it in the water," Duncan remembered. "I couldn't see exactly what he was up to but I was getting pretty annoyed with him for hanging around. I say he was 'hanging around' but he was probably not really all that long. I just wanted him gone."

Fleming looked at the back of the photograph.

"Thursday 3rd July 1980 at 4.55a.m. at Loch Leven." Fleming read.

"Yeah, what does anybody need to be there at that time for, anyone that isn't a photographer?" Duncan objected.

"Good question," said Fleming. "Want to help me answer it?"

"Just how might we do that?"

"By going back there tomorrow morning at the same time and finding the exact place this guy was at."

Duncan Hardisty wanted to laugh but he saw no sign of Fleming doing the same.

"You are serious, Andy? Five o'clock tomorrow morning?"

"We'll take my car, Duncan, unless you want to take the shot you tried to take back then."

"No, your car is fine by me. It won't break down or anything?"

"Always the pessimist Hardisty, have another dram."

At five the next morning Fleming drew into the lay-by beside Loch Leven. He asked Duncan to take the photograph to the spot where he had set up his camera in July 1980 and use it to shout directions to Fleming so that Fleming could place his car in exactly the same position as the Morris had occupied when the photograph had been taken.

When they had eventually achieved this, Fleming left his car and walked towards the water, again being directed by Duncan, he placed himself in the same spot once occupied by the Morris driver.

"Now Duncan, keep me right here as I walk towards the water. I want to end up where you saw this guy stop and spend some time, okay? I'm leaving a marker here in case I need to start over."

"Right, Andy, go forward, heading slightly to your right, no too much, keep it straighter." Duncan prompted. "That's better now, a little bit farther, about another five feet I think. Yes, that's perfect, where you're at now, stop."

"Okay Duncan, come on over here." Fleming shouted.

Duncan Hardisty ran over and burst out laughing. Fleming was standing in five inches of water.

"Sorry Andy, I guess the tide was out when the other guy did it."

"Perhaps," Fleming said, "But not necessarily, Duncan, look where you have brought me. I have this great slab of stone right in front of me. It must have been here for centuries."

"So?" Duncan replied with a puzzled look.

"So, I am going to lift it up and look underneath. You will need to be close enough to lift up anything we find underneath, right?"

Duncan Hardisty was not laughing now. He took off his shoes and socks and crept reluctantly into the cold water.

THE TALE OF THE OLD SCHOOL TIES

"I've no idea what to expect under here, Duncan, but if you see anything of any size at all, lift it away, okay?" Fleming urged. "I only hope I can lift this rock."

Fleming worked his fingers beneath the edge of the thick slab and pulled it slowly upwards. He was glad now to have left his shoes on his feet. As the rock broke from the hold of the sand and crushed shell in which it had lain for the past two years, Fleming found it easier to hoist. He was aware of Duncan leaping forward to grab something from beneath the rock.

"A black plastic parcel, Andy, look at this, it's like a wee football."

"Is that all there is, Duncan? I don't want to lift this again." Fleming said, concealing his elation but not his exertion.

"Yeah, that's all there is, Andy. It was sunk into the sand."

Fleming let the slab down gently.

"Right, Duncan, let's see what's in there. Bring it over to the dry grass."

"I don't like the feel of this thing, Andy. It's soft on the outside but firm underneath."

"We'll put it down first and open it on the grass." Fleming suggested.

Fleming had brought a small knife from his fishing gear and used it to cut the black bag just as close as he could to the cable tie seal. There was a smell from inside the bag as the trapped air escaped. Both men turned their heads away as the sides of the bag fell apart to allow an egress of water. When they looked back at the open parcel they saw a skull being supported by a nest of hair and a soup of degraded matter. Duncan Hardisty vomited involuntarily onto the sand and Fleming, despite the benefits of predisposition, struggled to avoid doing the same. He went to the water's edge and washed his hands. Duncan went to the water and washed his hands and face but remained in a crouched position facing the water.

"What now, Andy?" he asked quietly.

"Where's the nearest phone, Duncan?"

"The hotel just back round that corner beyond the bridge." Duncan answered.

Fleming took a piece of paper from his pocket. He had written the home number of Raymond Adam on it before he had left home that morning.

"Would you be all right to stay here with this, Duncan, if I went to the hotel and phoned?"

"Okay, just as long as I can keep this far away from it, Andy. Does this mean it is not coming back in the car with us?"

"That's what the phone call means, Duncan." Fleming said, laughing unkindly.

Fleming found the night porter at the hotel awaiting the bread roll and newspaper deliveries. He was granted use of the telephone and took the same sadistic pleasure in wakening Raymond Adam to break the news.

"So whose skull have you found?" Adam said dozily.

THE TALE OF THE OLD SCHOOL TIES

"I'm pretty sure it is Richard Barton, the boy from Letherford, two years ago." Fleming said confidently.

"Did you have to find it at five in the morning?" Adam asked in mock annoyance.

"That was the time of day that it was dumped here, sir." Fleming said.

"How the hell do you know – oh never mind. I'll be up there as soon as I can. I'll ring Campbell too. I'm not going to be the only one who needs to get up this early. You gonna stay with it 'til I get there?"

"Yeah, I'll probably do a bit of fishing." Fleming said cheekily. "I'll be here. Best bring a bucket to put this thing in, sir."

As he drove back to Duncan he smiled at the thoughts crossing his mind.

"Thanks Duncan, I've got things moving. Listen old son, take the car and get yourself home. Tell Mary what we found and say that I have to stay until the troops arrive."

Duncan had replaced his socks and shoes.

"You sure, Andy?"

"Just give me a minute, Duncan." Fleming said, going to the boot of his car. He returned with a carrier bag and a fishing rod.

"What's this?" Duncan asked with an expression of disbelief on his face.

"A couple of sandwiches and a can of Coke." Fleming said.

"And the fishing rod?"

"Well, I thought this kind of thing might happen."

"What if we had found nothing?" Duncan said.

"We would be half way home by now." Fleming said, shrugging his shoulders. "Oh, better give me that photo, Duncan. It'll help me to explain things."

It was shortly before seven when Raymond Adam arrived with Douglas Campbell and Darren Black. A Scenes of Crime officer arrived a few minutes later.

Adam and his CID colleagues looked in utter disbelief at the sight of Fleming standing at the water's edge tossing a baited hook and bubble float out into the loch. More surprising was the absence of any vehicle.

"Have you been here all night?" Adam asked.

"No sir, just since five." Fleming said, reeling in his line. "I gave Duncan my car to get home. Finding this didn't do the poor man much good." Fleming pointed to the black bag among the grass, a few feet away.

"Who's Duncan?" Darren asked.

"Duncan Hardisty, a professional photographer, he took this picture at five in the morning on the 3rd July 1980." Adam and Campbell had joined Darren at Fleming's shoulder to see the photograph. "At that time this car was owned by this man in the picture, Bert Jones, a man that none of us have actually seen. He bought the car on the 4th of June 1980; the wee boy whose skull is in that bag went missing on the 28th of June the same year. Jones got rid of the car to a William Menzies of Dumfries on the 12th of July again in 1980. Jones only had this car for as long as it took to do his first abduction and murder of a school child. I hope dental records will prove that this is Richard Barton."

Raymond Adam took the photograph from Fleming and turned it over to read the time and date on the reverse side. He smiled.

"So this is how you knew that it had been dumped at five in the morning." he said to Fleming.

"Taken by an independent witness with no knowledge of who this man was or what he was doing, you can't get much better than that." Fleming replied. "Ah, here comes my taxi." Mary had just drawn into the lay-by with his car. "See you guys at two."

"That was really very good Mrs Johns." the lady physiotherapist remarked after seeing her patient complete a set of leg bending exercises. "You must do these every morning if you are going to continue to live with these stairs of yours. If the knee gets worse it would mean living on one level or even a chair."

"No, there will be none of that nonsense," Valetta objected. "This has been my home for too long to be leaving it now. I will be exercising all day if I have to, but I am staying put with my house and my stairs."

Mary Ainsworth smiled. There was no point in arguing with Mrs Johns in her present mood and while she was still capable of climbing her stairs. The physiotherapist shook her head.

"I will be back in a week's time, Mrs Johns. I expect to see you doing as well as you did today," the girl said, turning to Mary, "same time next week."

When the girl had gone, Mary asked Mrs Johns how she felt about managing the stairs. Was she confident that she would not fall again?

"I haven't fallen yet" was the blunt reply.

Mary saw this as confirmation that the previous tumble downstairs had been assisted by her son but said nothing.

"You know, Mary, that young girl is just trying to tire me out with her fancy exercises. Who needs to peddle like that if they are not actually riding a bicycle?"

"That's a fair point," Mary said with a smile. "She may get you running up the stairs by the time she has finished."

"I have been here 42 years, Mary, and for me to run up those stairs for any reason, that would be a real first."

They both laughed.

Fleming arrived early for work that afternoon and went straight to the CID room. There he found Darren Black on his own. He heard from Darren how Raymond Adam and Douglas Campbell had left with the skull for the forensic mortuary. James Barrowman had been delighted by the discovery of the skull and was obtaining the dental records for Richard Barton.

"He has left a heap of court productions for you to sign, Andy, and that mate of yours will need to sign them as well but we can deal with that when we interview him."

THE TALE OF THE OLD SCHOOL TIES

"Here is my own statement, Darren. It will help you when it comes to interviewing Duncan and the Professor." Fleming said, handing a five page handwritten document to Darren.

"You wrote this today, since this morning?" Darren asked, with a hint of admiration.

"When you are busy like me, Darren, it is important to keep up to speed. I don't envy those people who are happy doing nothing, how do they know when they have finished?"

Darren laughed.

Their laughter attracted the attention of Chief Inspector MacKellar who entered the room to hand Fleming a small piece of paper. He then turned to Darren to ask about when Adam and Campbell expected to return. Fleming looked at the paper and read, 'Dick inbound 1 a.m.'

After hearing what Darren had to say about the skull going to Glasgow, MacKellar turned again to Fleming, "All right, Andrew?"

"No problem, sir"

MacKellar left and Fleming smiled.

"Did you hear that, Darren? I've just been promoted to Andrew."

As Fleming looked around the room his eye caught a cellophane bag labelled as a court production. The excess tape suggested it had been forensically examined before return to the CID.

"What is that thing?" Fleming asked Darren Black.

"That is the bone that Adam and Campbell took to be plaster rings. They found it in Jones' dustbin."

Darren brought it over to let Fleming see it. The bone had been cleaned and the rings placed in the correct sequence to show a reference number 144/54 in marker pen.

"I suppose it will just be going back to being rubbish, Andy. It's not the wee girl's plaster cast like Raymond Adam thought."

"Don't let them do that, Darren. I have a feeling it belongs to a museum. It is still evidence but it will have to wait for Mrs Halbooth to come home and identify it."

"Is it hers?" Darren said, looking puzzled.

"Only in a manner of speaking," Fleming replied. "But it links Bert Jones' to the green Morris car."

Sophie Rinstead had taken Mrs Ascot up on her invitation to return. She had gone first to Cynthia Ascot Johns' grave and laid fresh flowers.

Mrs Ascot was delighted to receive her young visitor and immediately invited Sophie in for tea. Sophie told Mrs Ascot about her scary experience at home and asked Mrs Ascot if she had happened to see Harvey Johns recently.

"No dear, he would have no interest in me. The way his mind works, I doubt that I ever enter his thoughts. I think you and your friend, Lorna, would be his primary targets. Lorna has been replaced in her absence by her poor mother."

THE TALE OF THE OLD SCHOOL TIES

"The police are looking for him, you know, but I think he is moving about quite a bit. I only hope he doesn't come back near my flat." said Sophie, her concern all too obvious in her voice.

"It is not at all rational," Mrs Ascot said, "to be going after people in revenge when it has been so long after the original events."

"Perhaps he has been in prison or something. We don't know where he has been since we last knew anything about him?" Sophie wondered.

"Yes, prison or some mental establishment would explain his disappearance certainly. In either case he would be better returned."

Before she left for the evening, Mary Ainsworth demonstrated to Mrs Johns how to set the security alarm and reminded her not to go out to feed the birds. That had been done. She also told her how to unset the alarm but she could leave that for Mary to do in the morning if she so wished. Mrs Johns set and unset the alarm several times for Mary's peace of mind before Mary left.

"What would happen if I set it off, Mary?" she asked with concern.

"There would be flashing lights and a siren loud enough to waken the neighbourhood." Mary told her.

"Oh dear, I had better be careful."

"You set it as soon as I leave. I will wait outside and you knock on the door from the inside when you have done it. I do not want you wandering off to the toilet and then forgetting whether you had set it or not."

"All right, Mary. Let's give that a try."

Mary left when Mrs Johns knocked on the door. It was giving the old lady some pleasure, this new game. She ran through to her television set and she could see Mary walking away from the front door. It was good to feel safe in her own home again and Valetta climbed the stairs, taking all the time she needed. There was no-one to spy on her capability. She walked into the second bedroom where everything always looked exactly as it had the day before. She went into the large walk-in cupboard that had once served as a wardrobe and saw the large cardboard box marked 'Wesley'.

She opened the top of the unsealed box and gently lifted out the Brigadier's splendid helmet, the one that her husband had worn so handsomely on ceremonial occasions. Beneath the helmet was the folded uniform, taking up the width and breadth of the box with rows of medal ribbons. Valetta was puzzled. She was sure that there had been a white lanyard lying on top of the uniform the last time she had looked in this box. Carefully she lifted up the folded jacket and trousers, not allowing them to lose their compact shape. Underneath them she was relieved to see her husband's service pistol and holster.

Sophie and Mrs Ascot enjoyed their meal together and afterwards spoke freely on many subjects, leaving the sour

THE TALE OF THE OLD SCHOOL TIES

matter of Harvey Johns to one side for the time being. Finding each other to be such pleasant company, neither had realised how quickly the evening was passing and Sophie was much later than she had intended to be. Summer time or not the light was beginning to fade as she said 'Goodnight' to Mrs Ascot and began her drive home.

Harvey Johns realised that his silver car was now known to Sophie Rinstead and as a result was probably the subject of police interest. For that reason he chose to park in the street behind the private blocks of flats where Sophie stayed. He could walk through to her block easily from there. As he locked his car, two teenage boys in hooded jackets offered to 'look after' it for him. He told them that it wouldn't be necessary as he would only be gone for a moment. He walked through the public pathway that led to the block of flats where Sophie lived. As soon as he was out of sight, the teenage boys sprayed black matt paint onto the lens glass of his car headlights.

Johns climbed the stairs inside the flats after seeing no sign of Sophie's car in the car park. He waited on the landing above Sophie's door and watched the car park through a stair window. He saw Sophie arrive and park her car. He smiled as he watched her look nervously around the car park for the silver car and he had to duck back from the window as she looked up at the building. He heard her come into the stairwell and noticed how every little sound was amplified by the emptiness of the common staircase. Her footsteps seemed loud and he could tell exactly where she was without looking. She was fumbling in a bag for her keys, he could tell that too. As she turned the key in the Yale lock he ran down to her level and pounced at her, pushing her inwards through the door of her flat. Sophie screamed and it sounded as loud as any siren due to the open doorway and the 'amplifier' of a staircase.

It was late enough for Todd Russell to be home and catching up with some recorded football. He heard the scream and immediately thought of Sophie Rinstead. He took a quick look out of his own window and saw Sophie's car. It had not been there when he had come home but it was there now. He rushed out of his own door and down the 'V' of stairs to the level below.

Harvey Johns had heard Todd's door opening and released Sophie, taking with him the white cord he had looped around her neck. Again he ran from a pursuing Todd Russell who shouted to Sophie to 'call the cops', as he paused by her door just long enough to see that she was conscious and responsive.

Sophie dialled 999 and told the police that she had been attacked again by the man in the silver car.

Todd Russell ran after the fleeing figure of Harvey Johns who lost sight of him as Harvey Johns turned down the public footpath. As Todd emerged into the dimly lit street at the other end of the footpath he saw the silver car moving away at speed, without lights, just as before.

THE TALE OF THE OLD SCHOOL TIES

He jogged back to Sophie's flat just as the police were arriving. He explained to the police driver that the assailant had just left the street behind them driving a silver car without lights. The police officer called in by radio to pass this information to others in the area and another car responded to the effect that it would try to head off the silver car at the exit from the housing scheme.

The police accompanied Todd as he went to Sophie's flat where the young woman was shaking with fear, her hand on her neck where the withdrawal of the cord had left a red line. Todd apologised for losing the attacker for a second time but suggested that the man's luck could not last forever. Sophie smiled at him and said nothing about her own luck.

"We already have him on our radar," one of the officers said. "His name is Bert Jones."

"No," Sophie protested. "It's not Bert Jones, it is Harvey Johns. I recognised him this time."

The second police car was single-crewed as it headed for the roundabout where all traffic exiting the estate would eventually show up. The entire area was well served by street lighting and the police officer saw the silver car travelling onto the roundabout at excessive speed from his left. The silver Ford turned left to travel directly ahead of the police vehicle.

The police driver switched on his blue lights and siren to pursue the Ford, simultaneously reporting by radio that he had the silver car in sight. Harvey Johns increased his speed as he realised that he was being pursued by a police car. On the straight well-lit main road he could expect to be caught quite easily and chose to turn off onto a branch road where he hoped to maintain his speed without the same opportunities for the police to overtake him. After two hundred yards the street lighting stopped and the Ford plunged into the darkness as Harvey Johns wondered at his own very poor headlights. For some reason they were not nearly strong enough to illuminate the road ahead. He braked savagely, he swerved, the car vaulted the roadside fence into a field and everything cut out. The police car stopped at the scene but the officer could see nothing in the field except small reflections caused by his own blue lights. He called in the crash of the silver car and asked for assistance.

Harvey Johns was battered and bruised but not badly hurt. Holding a new flashlight, formerly owned by Morton Grant, he left the car fully expecting a foot race with the police and sprinted off directly across the field, ignoring the darkness.

The police now had his silver car and they would stay with it until daylight, at which time they would impound the vehicle to a police garage.

Andrew Fleming went to his usual spot by the airstrip and parked without lights. He opened his window slightly to listen for the rotor blades and the sound arrived with military precision at exactly 1 a.m. The helicopter touched down on the tarmac and the single figure of the military intelligence officer ran to Fleming's car.

Once Dick was aboard, Fleming switched on his lights and saw the helicopter lift off.

"Drive away as usual, Andy." Dick said. "These guys will be watching for that."

"Yep," Fleming replied.

Two miles down the road there was a large lay-by overlooking the waters of a sea loch.

"Pull in here, Andy." Dick said. "We talk outside the car."

Andy smiled but did as he was told. He had seen this level of precaution before. He just hadn't seen it here.

The two men stood in silence, leaning against the car and becoming accustomed to the minimal light available. Registering the ambient noise levels was important too. If things changed they would simply leave without a word being said.

"I will tell you one story out here and then I will tell you another when we are back inside the car and on the move," Dick said quietly but distinctly. "I want you to merge both tales into one and there can be no questions regarding the first story, okay?"

"Roger."

"In the Second World War, the allies were moving north in Italy, heading for Cassino and Rome. The Americans were on the west of the peninsula, the British eighth on the east. The British met a river across their path but two infantry units crossed the river during nightfall and progressed towards the nearest village, part of the German Volturno line, where they took opposite sides of the village for their advance. Our account concerns only the eastern advance where a major was leading about one hundred and ten men. The major was older than normal for an operational officer, having been a boy soldier in the First World War in France. The village was well fortified by the axis forces with orders to stall the allies, east and west, while an even greater fortified resistance was being set up by the Germans a little farther north. For the Major's men there was no possibility of armoured reinforcement immediately, due to the river. They met the resistance of a greater force than expected at the village and were taking heavy casualties from machine gun fire. Three young soldiers are said to have turned from their forward position and ran back towards the major, perhaps to report what lay ahead, we'll never know. The major was in a highly agitated state and it is reported that he called these soldiers 'cowards' and 'deserters' and personally shot them down. One of the men shot down was Marcus Greenwell, the youngest of three brothers from Kent. The unit fought throughout the night and by morning had lost all but thirty of its total number. Of that thirty only two could tell the story I've just told you, but neither were believed, at least not officially. Their accounts lived on by word of mouth and the major was withdrawn from active service. There is no written record of this

THE TALE OF THE OLD SCHOOL TIES

story. The major survived and went on beyond the war to become a brigadier. He was married with a son called Bertram. Now let's get back in the car."

When the pair were under way, Fleming increased his average speed to make up for lost time and that drew no comment from Dick.

"You know that I once attended Letherford School, Andy," Dick began in pleasant conversational tones. "Well one year our prize-giving day was attended by a Brigadier Wesley Johns. He was a tall erect gentleman who suited the uniform remarkably well. He looked every inch a soldier and he cut quite a dash with the boys at the school. We were not aware of any problem but the brigadier was never asked back. It was whispered that he would not be allowed to set foot on the school grounds. We left school without knowing why this was the case but of course it had no real effect on any of us. Like most rules and policies the matter had been decided at Trustee level. The chairman of the board of trustees at that time was the father of the present chairman and one of three local brothers."

Dick stopped as if he had just told a child's fairy tale and had reached the end. He waited for a few moments before looking at Fleming. If his stories had been misunderstood there would be some facial indication to that effect. Fleming smiled.

"Quite a school, this Letherford, Dick, what was the school tie like? What were the colours?" Fleming asked in the same conversational tone.

"Oh, we had, and they still have, dark green blazers with a gold edge. The tie is dark green with a narrow diagonal gold stripes."

"I suppose you had to carry name labels on your clothes like they do today?"

"Yes, it is a real test of one's sewing ability to tack that label up inside a school tie, let me tell you."

"Was there a school motto?" Fleming asked.

"'Volens et potens' – willing and able." Dick replied as Fleming drew into the rendezvous point.

"Let's hope that applies to your next chauffeur, Dick. Here he comes." Fleming said cheerfully as the lights of an approaching car flashed briefly and the driver indicated his intention to enter the same lay-by.

"If you clear up this Letherford business, Andy, you may receive an honorary recognition from the school. Not really my suggestion, but an honourable gentleman whose word is law at Letherford."

"If I give you my measurements could he stretch to a blazer?" Fleming asked cheekily. Dick laughed as he climbed from the car. "Get out of here, Fleming."

As he drove back home, Fleming thought of what Dick had told him, 'we had a visit from an old Brigadier called Wesley Johns who was married and had a son called Bertram Johns'. Fleming paused as he realised the phonetic resemblance of Bert(ram) Johns and Bert Jones. Anyway this army officer had lost it in the heat of battle against superior numbers and had shot three of his own men dead, only one of whom, Marcus Greenwell, was worthy of a mention in Dick's version. Marcus Greenwell had been one of three Kent brothers and the present chairman of the school was the son of another. The man whose word was law around Letherford was presumably the present chairman of the board of trustees. To find this Bertram Johns would be easier if his parents address was known but were they still alive? Just how does one find an old brigadier?

Fleming arrived home at 2 a.m. but sleep did not come readily. After thirty minutes he rose and went to the copy newspapers he had received from young Anthony Halbooth. He read again the accounts of complaints from female pupils at Mary Upton School against a science teacher called Harvey Johns. The teacher was mentioned frequently but on only one occasion was referred to as B. Harvey Johns. Could that 'B.' stand for Bertram?

It was close to four in the morning before Fleming got to sleep.

NINE

When Fleming began work that afternoon, he found that Campbell and Black had been called away to assist DCI Raymond Adam. There had been dramatic developments in the Morton Grant murder case.

Bert Jones had been pursued by police following an attempt by him to strangle a 25 year old woman in Warwickshire. Jones had abandoned his crashed car in a country area and made his escape on foot but his vehicle was in the possession of the local police. Apparently all three CID men had set off for Warwickshire where they would be joined by Barrowman and Howell from Kent and Surrey.

Fleming felt deflated. His mind was awash with useful knowledge of this case and he had nobody to talk to about it. He hoped that the recovered car would give up some answers for Raymond Adam, but obviously Johns was still out there.

Fleming elected to visit Anthony Halbooth. The boy said that he still had the telephone number for the Surrey news editor he had spoken to.

It was mid-afternoon when the CID trio arrived in

THE TALE OF THE OLD SCHOOL TIES

Warwickshire. Darren Black had done most of the driving with Adam and Campbell both falling asleep for an hour or so. When they found the police station where the car was being held, they also found Barrowman and Howell waiting for them.

After introductions had been made, all five CID men heard of the local events that had led to the car chase and the recovery of the crashed Ford. They also heard how the pursuit had followed an attempted strangulation of Sophie Rinstead by a man that she knows to be Harvey Johns. The same man who had been living and working at Corran Bay as Bert Jones. This was the second time the man had attacked Sophie Rinstead since he had left Corran Bay. On both occasions the woman had been saved by a heavily built neighbour, otherwise she could reasonably have expected to die. Her attacker was still at large. Raymond Adam's murder suspect and Barrowman and Howell's murder and abduction suspect, Bert Jones or Harvey Johns, was still at large.

"We have looked at this car but we haven't explored it all, Raymond," James Barrowman explained. "Our man crashed into a field as you know but he must have landed on his wheels. It is filthy outside but the insides look pretty clean."

"Yeah, apparently that is how he kept his car, a lot cleaner than any of us would like." Adam said. "We won't keep you boys back. If we can examine the car inside we will know if we have anything of significance to our murder case lying there."

The five men went out to the garage where the car had been deposited from a breakdown truck.

"Thankfully the driver left the keys in the ignition," Barrowman remarked as he unlocked the boot lid and allowed it to swing upwards.

"Where did he get a sledgehammer?" Adam asked Campbell, but it was Darren who answered.

"I think he stole that hammer from the old man Gray downstairs."

"Right, the rest is fairly obviously his equipment, another hacksaw, black plastic bags, a large chisel and cable ties. I don't see any trace of blood in here. That's encouraging."

"In what way?" Howell asked.

"No new victims being carried in the boot since he left home." Adam replied. "What about the car itself, Jim? Has he got anything up front?"

"Again pretty neat and tidy, Raymond, considering he has been living out of this car."

The Kent detective opened the driver's door and pointed at the inside with a shrug of his shoulders. There was nothing to see except a cardboard box which appeared, at first glance to contain tissues. Adam looked closer.

"Latex gloves, the kind they use in hospitals," he observed.

"Or laboratories," Douglas Campbell suggested, turning to Barrowman. "Johns has been working in a laboratory."

THE TALE OF THE OLD SCHOOL TIES

Adam had moved round to the other side of the car where he pulled an AA road map from beneath the passenger seat. It was examined page by page but was unmarked and contained nothing in the way of notes. Raymond Adam opened the glove compartment. Lifting them by their edges and using his fingertips, he brought onto the passenger seat a batch of photographs and a notebook.

"Are these gloves of his all new, Dougie? If they are, give me a pair, will you?"

Campbell pulled the top two from the box and gave them to his boss. Raymond Adam put on the gloves before lifting the photographs, one by one and still by their edges despite the use of gloves. He took each one from the pile separately and showed them to his colleagues.

"These are just snaps of pieces of ground with nothing special about them. Here is one of a river bank. This one is of a smashed headstone," Raymond Adam sighed. "I don't see the point of these at all and yet there must be a relevance. Let's see what this book has to offer."

He lifted the notebook and turned each page with the closed end of his pen.

"We have a list of names and addresses here," he said, sounding more hopeful.

"Do you boys know any of these people? Lorna Templeton, Sophie Rinstead, well we do know about her, Mrs Valetta Johns and Lord Brackston."

Dennis Howell raised his hand and spoke out, "Lorna

Templeton and Sophie Rinstead were the two young girls who made a complaint of having been sexually molested at school by a science teacher called Harvey Johns. That was at the Mary Upton School for Girls, ten years ago."

"So who will Mrs Valetta Johns be? His mother?" Adams asked.

"I think that will prove to be his mother, Chief Inspector. His father is dead, I am told." Howell recalled from what he had read during school enquiries into the Holloway abduction. "Nobody had any idea where to look for Harvey Johns back then."

"I think that is still the way of things." Adam said with a smile.

"Lord Brackston is the chairman of our Board of Trustees at Letherford School. I should know. The man has been on my back a fair bit." Barrowman added.

Raymond Adam raised a finger and drew it back and forth between Barrowman and Howell.

"This supports a connection between your cases, gentlemen. This character that we are looking for wrote these names in this book, not any of us. He is the common culprit. He has just told us so."

"So his name is certainly Johns and not Jones," Barrowman said. "And that list is of people against whom he bears a grudge. I know that Mrs Johns was attacked in her own home recently. There was a telex message to that effect. Is there anything else in there, Raymond?"

Not a lot, just empty pages for the most part, but here

is another list. It looks like racehorses, 'Lionheart', 'Leven Sand', 'Trojan Lady', 'Black Bear's Path', Blacksmith's son' and 'Claddick Point'. Does that mean anything to you?"

"I don't think they are racehorses, Raymond," Barrowman said. "I know my horses and I've never seen any of these names before. They could be greyhounds of course."

Darren Black had ideas of his own but, being the junior member of the group, kept quiet. A constable from the station ran out to the group, "Detective Chief Inspector Adam?"

"That's me." Raymond told him.

"There is a call from Corran Bay, sir, an Andrew Fleming."

"Oh, right son, I'll be right in," Adam told the young constable. "Excuse me, gentlemen."

Darren Black and Douglas Campbell exchanged looks. Only Darren smiled.

"Who's Andrew Fleming?" Barrowman asked, having sensed the unspoken humour between the pair.

"A cross between Sherlock Holmes and Billy the Kid," Campbell replied, making Darren Black smile even more.

Raymond Adam re-joined the group.

"Let's look in that boot again, gentlemen. According to Fleming there should be a carpet plug missing," he reported, opening the boot himself. He checked around the edge of the boot carpet himself and found the plugs to be present and correct, all except one. Raymond Adam lifted the carpet and searched around the boot and spare wheel well without finding the missing plug. There just was not one there.

"Damn the man," Adam said aloud.

"Where is the plug, sir?" Darren Black asked.

"You know where it will be. That bugger has it in his pocket. He found it on the road at the bridge on the Sunday afternoon following Morton Grant's murder. It was lying beside the bridge parapet. He knew it 'would come in handy', he says." Adam was grunting to himself as he replaced the boot carpet, not stopping to notice that the smiling faces had increased to four.

"Do you want to take this car north, Raymond? You are the man with the proven murder case," James Barrowman asked.

"It would need to be taken to Glasgow and then transported all the way south again to London for your cases, Jim," Raymond Adam thought aloud. "I'll take the contents with me. They may help us with identification of them by witnesses, if not, we can always send them south to you without too much expense. I think they will be germane to both your cases in due course, fair enough?"

Barrowman and Howell nodded.

"Dougie, make out production labels for the items from the boot, these photographs, the box of gloves and the notebook. Jim, Dennis, you men will want to examine the car forensically for any trace of your missing kids. If

THE TALE OF THE OLD SCHOOL TIES

you come across invisible blood traces in that boot and they do not connect to the children then there is a good chance that the blood will have belonged to our victim, Morton Grant. According to Fleming Jones or Johns or whatever his name is, washed the boot carpet that Sunday morning."

Barrowman's eyes opened wide and he was tempted to ask how Fleming would have known that but he decided against asking.

"That first missing boy, Richard Barton, won't have been in that car, I expect. Fleming says that Jones owned a different car at that time and he suspects that the skull that we have is from that wee fellow. Dental records for Richard Barton, Jim, did you manage to obtain them?"

"I brought them Raymond. They are in the police office here. I remembered to bring them," Barrowman said cheerily. "I hope Billy the Kid is right."

Raymond Adam drew him a strange look.

"I never realised that you would be at home," Penelope Halbooth said to her husband, almost apologetically. "It was rather heavily suggested that we all take a break to visit our respective homes and I had to bow to the greater demand. It is scarcely the same with depleted numbers anyway."

"All right, Penelope, you have made your point but I think you ought to be pleased to see your son when you have the chance to know what a healthy and intelligent boy he has become. I cannot understand why the boy would have to become a fossil before you would be interested." Milton Halbooth said quite venomously.

"The boy has his own life to lead, his own path to follow, Milton." Penelope retorted.

"'The boy' is over here, mother, sitting in this very room," Anthony spoke up from his armchair. "You are speaking about me as if I had already reached some inanimate state. I am quite conscious of having my own life to lead and path to follow and I may well choose a rather different one from my parents."

"Oh, and what would that be, Anthony?" his father asked.

"I will have to take a closer look at the subject before deciding, but I think that criminal psychology may well be suited to my talents." he said in a positive way.

"You are simply displaying mischief." his mother said, obviously not amused.

"There may be a greater need for criminal psychologists than for Latin interpreters or poets," his father said more quietly.

"Everything is down to money with you, Milton," Penelope objected.

"Am I to suppose, Penelope, that you are scratching about in the earth for nothing?" he replied in the same quiet, but annoying, manner.

Penelope turned again to her son.

"You should do what you want to do, Anthony, but

THE TALE OF THE OLD SCHOOL TIES

with an intellect like yours there can be more to life than the criminal activity of others. As your father should be telling you, crime does not pay."

Just at that moment someone knocked on the house door and Penelope, who was closest to the door, looked at it as if trying to recall what action required to be taken when this occurred.

She went to the door and opened it to find Constables Andrew Fleming and Hamish MacLeod.

"Good afternoon, Mrs Halbooth, I am so glad to find you at home. It is actually yourself that I have come to see." Fleming said with a smile.

"What have I done?" Penelope asked with no feeling of guilt, just an awareness of how prone she was to catastrophic accidents.

"You have not done anything wrong, Mrs Halbooth. I simply want you to recognise something for me," Fleming said, making Milton and Anthony curious. "I have in here a sawn-up bone which may well have been in your possession at one time. Do you recognise this?" he asked, lifting a clear cellophane bag that contained the bone segments in sequence so that the number 144/54 was visible.

"That bone is from the Natural Science Museum," she said. "Someone has stolen it and cut it into pieces."

"Well, not exactly, Mrs Halbooth," Fleming said, wishing that he did not have to contradict this lady. "We believe that it was left in the old Morris car that you were driving back and forth when you were working for the museum. It was in the possession of the man who bought the Morris from Professor Halbooth."

"Oh, you're right, there was a piece missing," Penelope Halbooth remembered excitedly. I had no idea where it was. That will be it. I could check with the museum if you wish but they will not be pleased to have it back cut into rings."

"In that case we will settle for your identification of the bone. For our purposes it proves one or two points of evidence." Fleming assured her. We will simply take a statement from you to the effect of what you have said and we would ask you to sign this label. The item will remain with us as evidence in a case against the man who bought the car."

"How exciting," Penelope said, lifting her hands up in front of her in the manner of a meerkat.

As the officers noted her statement, Penelope Halbooth became more excited to learn that Anthony had become a friend of Andrew Fleming and had actually assisted with some serious criminal matters.

"He is thinking of becoming a criminal psychologist, you know," she said proudly.

"Anthony would be excellent in that profession," Fleming assured her.

Milton Halbooth and Anthony exchanged looks of disbelief.

On the return journey north Raymond Adam and Douglas Adam speculated on the English cases while

THE TALE OF THE OLD SCHOOL TIES

Darren Black sat quietly in the back seat without being consulted too often. He grew tired of listening to the constant 'if's and 'could's and 'maybe's coming from his colleagues and looked out of the window for interest. The traffic flow became lighter and Darren turned his attention to the photographs and notebook lying beside him on the back seat. He dared not touch them but he thought about two of the terms on the list at the back of the book. He had heard of 'Black Bears Path' and 'Claddick' point, or more correctly Claddich Point. Both were places on a tourist map, he was sure of it. Beyond these items lay the brown envelope containing the dental records of a twelve year old boy who had disappeared in 1980.

Darren considered the grief of the parents and how they might feel if the skull from Loch Leven proved to their son. What would it mean to them to have only their son's head to bury?

Raymond Adam broke his journey to Corran Bay to hand in the dental records and the hacksaw to the crime laboratory. He asked for urgent examination and comparison with the skull they already had.

The trio were extremely tired by the time they reached Corran Bay. Darren had driven the last 90 miles and had no more thoughts on the murder cases or the victims. He was struggling to stay alert.

Andrew Fleming saw the CID group arrive and was anxious to hear what had been learned. They were just not in the mood to be telling him.

"Will you be here tomorrow, sir?" he asked Adam.

"You tell me, Fleming. You are the bugger with all the answers." Adam said huffily, his mood down to exhaustion.

"In that case you will be," Fleming said cutely.

"What for?" Adam said with impatience.

"To go back to 24 Heather Road with me, sir," Fleming suggested.

"We have already used the search warrant, Fleming and we never found anything to go back for."

"What about the guy's clothes?" Fleming asked.

"What about them? They were all clean and dress stuff. Are you suggesting that he put on a suit to kill Morton Grant?" Adam said, obviously frustrated in his fatigue. "We are not entitled to take his clothes unless we have evidential reasons for doing that. What reasons do you suppose there are?"

"I just want to put a consideration to rest, sir. Can you go back there tomorrow morning?"

Adam thought for a moment. Fleming could see just how knackered Adam felt at the moment and tomorrow morning Fleming himself would be off-duty again. He would not push his luck with Adam unless he had good reason. Whatever it was, Adam knew that he would only become privy by conceding.

"You are off tomorrow morning but you are prepared to come in to do this?" he asked Fleming in a more conciliatory tone.

"That's right," Fleming replied immediately,

understanding Adam's thoughts as clearly as if the man had spoken them out loud.

"Then we will all go. I will get that Housing Association guy to come as well. We are just looking, right?"

"And if we find evidence?" Fleming pushed.

Adam drew a deep breath.

"I'll consult the Fiscal at nine in the morning. I want to ask him if he wants that wrecked car anyway. You lot be here at nine-thirty.

They turned to go.

"Oh Fleming," Adam said, said holding out his hand. "Give me that damn carpet plug."

James Barrowman had wasted no time in having a forensic team go over the silver car belonging to Bert Jones, or Harvey Johns as he was now known to be.

Fibres taken from the seemingly clean carpet of the boot were alien to the vehicle upholstery and initial examination suggested a consistency of colour with the known colours of school uniform material worn by pupils of Letherford and Mary Upton Schools. Further microscopic examination might substantiate an identical likeness. Just as Raymond Adam had suggested, the boot mat still had invisible traces of human blood. The blood trace was singular and would probably be that of the Scottish victim, Morton Grant. Within the passenger compartment of the vehicle fibres were also found in deep green, deep pink and grey. The upholstery of the car was grey but these particular fibres were darker. The fibres were few in number but had been so embedded in the fabric of the car seats and carpet as to have survived all attempts to vacuum or brush them away. Barrowman could imagine the desperate efforts of a bound child trying to free himself or herself from tape or rope.

A single human hair was found lying along a metal seam in the boot of the car. It was not consistent in colour with either child and may have belonged to Morton Grant. Later examination would reveal the presence of blood on the same hair.

Barrowman and Howell organised another urgent circulation in the hunt for Harvey Johns. There was no up-to-date photograph of the wanted man but a media broadcast was made with a description. Sophie Rinstead had given her description to a police sketch artist in order to create an artistic impression of the fugitive. Mrs Valetta Johns read about her son in the newspaper, not for the first time. Mary Ainsworth had tried to insist on staying over with Valetta 24 hours a day, but Mrs Johns would not hear of it. This was a family problem, why should Mary be exposed to any danger?

Fleming arrived early at the police office and found Douglas Campbell and Darren Black waiting for Raymond Adam to return from a discussion with the Procurator Fiscal. The CID officers described the previous day's trip to England and told Fleming about the contents of the silver Ford.

"What would Johns have wanted with old Tom Gray's sledgehammer?" Fleming wondered.

"No idea," said Douglas Campbell. "The big chisel is probably for gaining entry but we don't know that he has actually used it anywhere. That hacksaw might tell us more, I fancy."

"What about this notebook?" Fleming asked.

Douglas Campbell donned a pair of gloves and opened the book to show Fleming the list of names and addresses.

"These are people he holds a serious grudge against, Andy. The English cops reckon they are all in danger."

Fleming pulled a sheet of paper from his inside pocket and began to compare it with the notebook.

"What's that?" Campbell asked.

"A copy of Jones' application for the job at the lab," he said. "I am comparing the handwriting. It looks the same to me."

Campbell took a deep breath.

"Don't mention that to Adam," he advised earnestly. "He's mad enough already. Here is the list of greyhounds." Campbell said, smiling as he turned to the back page and winking to Darren Black.

Fleming looked at the list for a few moments and reached for the photographs but Campbell stopped him. "I'll lift them, Andy."

"I think I see what these are about," Darren Black volunteered.

"Good for you, Darren," Fleming said with a smile. "Start at the top."

"Well, that Leven Sand is where you found the skull, Andy."

"Right." said Fleming.

"And I think that 'Black Bear's Path' is part of the nature trail near Kinlochleven."

"Yep." said Fleming. "And Claddich Point is a viewing spot overlooking Loch Awe."

"What about Lionheart?" Campbell asked.

"I am guessing that they are not places but the people concerned as victims whose heads are buried at the given locations," Fleming said. "The Lionheart would be Richard as in Richard the Lionheart and Richard Barton, appropriately beneath 'Leven Sand'; Trojan Lady would be Helen of troy and Helen Holloway and the Blacksmith's son is a reference to Faraday as in William Faraday and Michael Faraday the scientist whose father was a blacksmith."

"Why would he leave this cryptic stuff?" Campbell asked. "Surely he would remember them well enough?"

Fleming was now looking at the photographs, laid out in a fan by Campbell.

"Same reason he left these pictures of the places he is referring to," Fleming guessed. "He knows he has a problem. He has provided these for anyone who takes enough interest to catch up with him. This man is not altogether stupid, but he is completely mad. Maybe he knows that."

THE TALE OF THE OLD SCHOOL TIES

At that moment Raymond Adam came back to the room holding a paper.

"Sorry to keep you boys, the Fiscal got a new warrant, so we had better not be wasting our time, Fleming."

"I'm the only one whose time can be wasted, sir. The rest of you are getting paid, remember?"

"Aye right," said Adam. "Well, we best get going. The Housing Association chap will be waiting for us up at Heather Road. Have you got Mr Gray's hammer, Dougie?"

"Yes sir," Campbell replied. "Is he getting it back?"

"No. It is still evidence until we know otherwise. Just get his signature on that label if he identifies it."

Tom Gray did identify his hammer and was surprised to hear that it had been to England in the boot of Jones' car.

The police officers and housing agent entered the flat at No. 24 and Adam turned to Fleming.

"Okay, smartass, what did we miss?" he asked unkindly.

"I don't know yet, but let's look at his clothes," Fleming suggested, crossing to the bedroom and heading for the wardrobe.

He opened the wardrobe doors and behind one there was a fitted tie bar. Hanging over the bar were upwards of a dozen ties of all description. Fleming began to tease them apart with his fingers and pulled out one in dark green with diagonal gold stripes. He then found another tie that was identical to the one he had. From the remainder he took out a tie in pink and grey. He turned to face the others as they watched with interest.

"The dark green and gold ties belong to pupils of Letherford School. The pink and grey one belongs to a young lady from Mary Upton School for Girls."

"How do you know that?" Campbell asked, a little annoyed at himself for having paid scant attention to this tie rack.

"Because I asked," Fleming said simply. "The uniform recovered from the waste bin at the service station following William Faraday's abduction did not include the school tie."

He carefully inverted the broad end of the tie, the newer of the two, to reveal a name tag sewn inside with the name 'William J. Faraday'.

"Well done, Andy," said Raymond Adam with a wide smile and a new found favour for his favourite 'smartass'.

Fleming inverted the broad end of the second Letherford tie to show a name tag with the name 'Richard Barton' inside. The pink and grey tie had a similar tag neatly sewn inside which read, 'Mary Upton School – Pupil No. 52'.

"I think this belongs to our Trojan Lady." Fleming remarked.

"Would he just keep these ties as trophies, do you suppose?" Darren asked, to nobody in particular.

"Trophies and possible murder weapons," Fleming said with confidence.

"Why murder weapons?" Adam asked without criticism.

"His chosen method of attack, apparently," Fleming replied. "Especially if you choose to believe that his wife did not commit suicide."

Raymond Adam turned to his Detective Sergeant.

"See what you missed, Mr Campbell?"

Fleming was looking in the drawer that held socks and checked them all for name tags but there were none. He then looked at the three suits.

"You checked the pockets, Dougie?" he asked rhetorically.

"I did." Campbell replied. Fleming closed the doors as if Campbell's word was good enough.

"I think we have what we came for," Fleming told Raymond Adam. "That was the consideration that was bothering me. It was actually something that Dougie said."

Fleming did not enlighten anyone further. He only enjoyed Campbell being criticised when he was doing it himself.

They returned to the police station and Raymond Adam took great delight in phoning James Barrowman with his news of the latest discoveries.

"We are hoping to do some digging, Jim. Our man Fleming reckons the skulls of the other two children are buried at certain places up here. That was what that list of 'greyhounds' was all about. I'll get back to you on that and the result of the dental comparison. I might well get that today."

TEN

Black Bear's Path and Claddich Point were both several miles from Corran Bay and Fleming was not involved in surveying either location.

Raymond Adam was enjoying his investigation now as he took a small team to both locations. Each team possessed copies of the photographs taken by Harvey Johns and would use them to define the areas to excavate. Team members had been told what to expect and were warned to use the greatest of care. The earth had to be scraped rather than dug, especially if the ground had the appearance of having been disturbed. They also had riddles to use if necessary.

Douglas Campbell was left in charge at Black Bear's Path while Adam himself went to Claddich Point.

For both teams there was a problem with radio communication. The search sites were remote and, with the mountains around, there was no way to transmit or receive to/from each other or to any mutual base. This had been predicted and Raymond Adam provided both teams with the necessary equipment to record their finds and to convey their evidence in a satisfactory manner, back to

Corran Bay. If they were still busy when the light failed there would be a return the following day.

Fleming began work on his normal shift at 2 p.m. and teamed up with Hamish for a foot patrol among the gathering numbers of holiday-makers on the streets of Corran Bay.

"We are just overpaid tourist guides at this time of year," Hamish commented after they had given directions to the tenth tourist in a row.

"Would you rather be digging for a child's skull?" Fleming asked with a smile. He knew how much Hamish disliked dead bodies.

Hamish gave a shiver, "No. How can anybody do that to children, Andy?"

"They have to be mad to do it, Hamish and we would have to be mad to understand them doing it." Fleming answered. "I prefer the way we are."

When they came back to the office Fleming was spoken to by Chief Inspector MacKellar who congratulated him on his work with the Morton Grant case and the English abduction cases. MacKellar had never investigated any crime and had scarcely seen an angry man during his administrative career, but Fleming found his change of tone refreshing. The conversation ended with the real reason for it occurring. He handed Fleming a small white envelope.

Fleming opened it and read, 'Dick outbound at midnight'.

"Okay Andrew?"
"Okay sir."

It was around 7 p.m. when Raymond Adam returned to the police office from Claddich Point. He carried a clear plastic bag containing a small skull that he placed in a box on a bed of crushed paper. The remains could equally well have been described as a 'head' for it was recently buried and still had the recognisable features of a young boy. Adam beckoned Andrew Fleming and Hamish MacLeod through to see the severed head. Hamish politely declined but Fleming went to see the effects of a month's burial on a human head.

"We are going to have to find somewhere cool to store this until I hear from the other crew." Adam said soberly.

"I think Mr and Mrs Faraday could just about identify their son." Fleming remarked.

"Aye, it was in peaty soil, Andy. It discolours a body but usually preserves it not too bad."

"Ice." said Fleming.

"What about it?"

"I'll get some from the ice factory on the pier. We only need enough to sit the box on top. That should keep it cool enough. We can keep it in the ladies toilet. The typists are finished."

It was another hour before Douglas Campbell and his team returned. They had dug in three different spots before uncovering a skull with hair still adhering to it. The head of Helen Holloway, lying on a bed of crushed paper, could more aptly be called a skull.

Charlie Macdonald could tell Raymond Adam that Mr McLay had called during the afternoon. The dental records had confirmed the identity of the first skull as that of Richard Barton.

"Good. I feel like a good drink," Adam exclaimed. "It has been a successful day. Do you suppose these two will keep 'til tomorrow morning, Dougie? Andy Fleming got the ice for them."

"I think they will keep better than I will," said Campbell, looking as tired as he sounded.

"Better put a notice on that toilet door, Charlie, to keep these typists out of that toilet until we take these heads away. I don't want to be responsible for some poor bugger's heart attack." Adam instructed.

When Andrew Fleming finished his late-shift he had too little time to go home and instead headed out to the rendezvous point to meet with Dick, after calling Mary to explain his lateness.

At midnight he saw the approaching patrol car flash its lights and pull into the lay-by. Dick emerged immediately and walked smartly across to Fleming's car.

As they drove away, Dick looked across at Fleming and asked, "Well?"

"The hounds are still pursuing their fox but there is no

longer a mystery. The fox is known. He has been working under two different names but his true name begins with the first name Bertram."

"Oh, I see. Then I have been of some assistance." Dick said with a nod of satisfaction.

"The fox is still a danger. He had a list of targets. We have his list and it includes the name of Lord Brackston. Do what you can to warn him, Dick, will you?"

"I will."

Fleming yawned involuntarily and apologised.

"Long hours, Andy?"

"Aye, something like that, the adrenalin drops and – well you know what it's like."

"Yes," Dick said with a laugh, "I've just become the most boring part of your day."

Andrew Fleming laughed.

"Just returning the favour, Dick, just returning the favour." Fleming said quietly. "By the time you cross the coast I'll be in my bed."

"I might still be asleep before you," Dick said with a yawn.

"Don't leave Lord Brackston until it's too late." Fleming reminded Dick as he dropped him off at the airstrip.

"I won't." Dick assured him. Fleming watched Dick until the helicopter lifted off into the night sky. He then headed home, not too jealous of his friend.

Sophie Rinstead's parents lived in Provence in France,

having moved there when Sophie had gone to university. They kept in touch by monthly telephone calls to their daughter but had been told nothing of the attacks made on Sophie by her one-time school teacher, Harvey Johns. They would have remembered Harvey Johns but had never learned the truth of the complaints lodged by their daughter and her friend, Lorna Templeton. Even in her remorseful and conscientious endeavour to tell Harvey Johns of her regret, she had not considered telling her own parents.

She had not seen them this year and after her nervous, broken sleep of the past few nights she felt very inclined to make the trip. Her enquiries with the ferry companies and the French rail network made it seem possible. She decided to go to Provence. Once there she would tell her parents the whole truth. If she was there beside them they would be assured of her safety. Hopefully by the time she returned to start a new term Harvey Johns would be in police custody and her life would be more settled.

She sat down and wrote a full airmail letter to Lorna Templeton explaining all that had happened and what her present intentions were.

"You do not have to watch these multiplex pictures all the time, Mrs Johns," the young man explained. "You should watch your own choice of channel and if the cameras are triggered then you will see a pulsating circle in the top left hand corner of the screen. You see I have put

THE TALE OF THE OLD SCHOOL TIES

it onto BBC 1 for now. Mrs Ainsworth, could you perhaps walk out onto the patio and that should trigger the camera there?"

Mary walked out through the patio doors and into the morning sunshine.

"There you are, Mrs Johns, do you see the pulsating circle there?"

"Yes, I do." Valetta replied.

"Do you think you would notice that? I can make it larger."

Valetta laughed.

"I will see it all right. The corner of my eye will be constantly watching for it, never fear."

Mary came back in. "Did it work?" she enquired.

"You were a star, Mrs Ainsworth," the young man from the security firm said with a chuckle. "You can be again. Would you mind going out again and I will allow Mrs Johns to react to the circle? Let's see how clearly the camera picks you up."

Mary went back outside and the young man gave Mrs Johns the control as the circle appeared again. Valetta pressed the red button to bring in the set of pictures and then button 2 to focus on the patio screen showing Mary in clear black and white detail.

"During the darkness your picture will be just as clear, believe me. The infra-red has been much improved," the security man promised her. "You seem to have mastered the controls very well. Never panic, remember. Stay calm in adversity and you will capture the best picture available. Everything you see on screen will be recorded just as you have it on screen."

"I feel a lot more confident with it now, young man," Mrs Johns assured him, looking pleased with her own efforts.

"Let's hope she never really needs it." Mary Ainsworth said, returning from the patio.

"No, Mary, we could make our own movies instead."

That same morning Sophie had begun her journey by travelling into London by train and was now studying the large screen of train departures. The trains to Dover should be linked to the ferry timetable and the next train was due to depart in five minutes. She scurried to the ticket office and groaned at the sight of the queues. With scarcely a minute to spare she obtained her ticket and rushed off to the platform unaware of the rough looking man who had noticed her.

The unkempt figure reached down behind a litter bin and picked up a discarded ticket from the ground. He ran in frantic fashion towards the train he had just seen Sophie boarding.

The doors were about to close, guards were scanning the platform, whistles were being blown and a railway guard stood in his path but Harvey Johns held up his ticket while pointing desperately at the train. It was easy to believe that a passenger bound for France would be anxious not to miss the train and the guard did not feel like rugby tackling this man. Johns boarded near the back of the train and the door was closed behind him.

The train was busy and Sophie was fortunate to find a seat beside a tall well-built gentleman. There were people in the aisle constantly, seeming always to be dissatisfied with their current position and needing to go elsewhere. Sophie watched this interchange of bodies and caught a glimpse of the unshaven man at the end of her carriage.

'It cannot be him,' she thought. 'How could I be this unlucky?'

There was no mistake. Harvey Johns was looking at each passenger in turn as he moved up the aisle, behaving almost like a ticket collector. He would certainly find Sophie. She felt that she must do something, but to leave her seat would be made obvious by the rush of others to occupy it. Once she was on her feet she would have to stay on the move trying to avoid Johns all the way to Dover.

She remembered that her windcheater had a hood. With her sports bag at her feet, she pulled her hood up to cover her head and turned to bury her face into the shoulder of the man beside her. He looked at her without annoyance.

"Are you all right?" he asked in English but with a French accent.

"I am being followed. Please help me to hide, please."

The big man could have been a rugby player or even a heavyweight boxer, but he caught the urgency in her voice and placed an arm around her shoulders, inviting her to sleep if she wanted to.

Harvey Johns paused to look briefly at Sophie. The grey garment looked much the same but the dark French eyes of the big chap with his arms around the girl were not familiar or welcoming. The girl must be his girlfriend, or so Harvey Johns believed. He moved on.

As he moved on through the train Harvey Johns failed to find anyone else who looked at all like Sophie Rinstead. How had she eluded him? Had she gone into a toilet?

Meantime, Sophie was explaining to her French saviour how her pursuer was a stalker who had twice attacked her physically in the past and she had not expected him to have followed her onto the train. She was going to Provence to visit her parents and she was afraid of being confined on a ferry. The genial Frenchman assured her that she would come to no harm. He was intending to use the ferry himself and she could continue to accompany him if she wanted. She could rely on his protection from this man if it was needed.

As the hordes of passengers disembarked at Dover, Sophie and her new friend, Marc, walked together without showing the least concern. Sophie was concerned enough, however, to keep her hood up. Harvey Johns had failed to see the woman he had recognised as Sophie Rinstead at the London platform and accepted that she had somehow escaped him. He left the rail terminal an angry and frustrated beast. Now he must find his way back to London.

THE TALE OF THE OLD SCHOOL TIES

DCI Raymond Adam had accompanied both of the recently recovered skulls to Glasgow for forensic examination. Dental records were available for Helen Holloway and William Johnston Faraday from the dentists under contract to the schools. These records were being sent north in the full expectation of the police that identification of the pupils would follow.

Before leaving that morning, Raymond Adam had spoken to both James Barrowman and Dennis Howell to apprise them of the previous day's events – the discovery of the skulls and the recovery under warrant of the school ties.

He had a secure case against this 'Bert Jones' or Harvey Johns, for the murder of Morton Grant.

"Why did he kill that man?" Barrowman had asked him.

Fleming had reckoned that Morton Grant had been painting the lamp-post outside Johns' flat in Heather Road, his work book had said so. Johns had been cutting up a bone with a saw. Morton may have seen that, perhaps, but what he did see was Johns coming out to his dustbin with a black plastic bag and when Johns had seen Morton looking at him, had decided against putting the bag into his bin. Morton, being the man he was, was curious to find out what the man at No. 24 was hiding. Later that night, with the encouragement to his imagination that five or six pints of beer could bring, Morton had gone to search that dustbin. Johns had come out and struck him from behind with a ballpeen hammer three times, killing him. He had taken him to the railway bridge and thrown him over, failing to notice that, as he had pulled the body from the boot of the car, he had also lifted out one of his carpet plugs. On his return to Heather Road, Johns had cleaned up his car.

Johns had no idea how much Morton Grant had seen from the top of his ladder but if Morton had reported it to the police then Johns would need to satisfy the police as to his innocence. To this end he had cut up the bone he had kept since finding it in the boot of the Morris.

He was ready for the police to respond to any report made to them by Morton Grant. What he had not expected was the return of Morton himself, at midnight on a Saturday night, to search his dustbin. In one of those unstable moments where circumstances seemed to overrun him, Johns had reacted with violence and murdered Morton Grant. At this point Fleming's version is supported by Tom Gray who heard Johns take something away in his car, something too big and heavy to go into the dustbin. Old Tom had heard Johns washing his car on his return.

Fleming had based his account on Harvey Johns' weakness in the face of adversity, reflecting his father's performance in Italy, although he chose to keep this knowledge to himself.

Raymond Adam smiled to himself. If anyone ever saw fit to murder Raymond Adam he would want Fleming to follow it up. Fleming, he knew, would make his own mind up on whether to do that or not. When he had suggested on two previous occasions that Fleming should apply for the CID, he had been told by Fleming that he never wore 'disposable suits' and preferred to work with those who never had to tell people that they were detectives.

Valetta Johns was finding her new security equipment quite entertaining and would switch on her television set to show Mary the postman delivering the mail.

"If I wanted to, Mary, I could zoom in and read the address on the letters he is carrying."

"Really?" said Mary, quite impressed.

"You try it Mary. Write something down on a piece of paper and take it outside without telling me what you wrote and I will read it with the zoom on the camera." Valetta urged. "When you come back in, I will tell you what you wrote."

Mary did as she was asked and wrote on a scrap of paper, 'the temperature today is 23 degrees Celsius'. She went outside and held it towards the camera. Valetta zoomed in and read the note.

"All right, Mary," she laughed. "It is too warm to be inside watching television."

She switched the set off and walked slowly out to the summer seat, making good use of her walking stick. Mary brought out cool drinks for them both.

"There is still no word of Harvey," Mary said, unsure

of the wisdom of doing so, but conscious of Mrs Johns' private concern.

"I don't know if the police would tell me whether they had him or not." Valetta said pensively.

"I would expect that the papers would have the story," Mary suggested. "They have said everything else there was to say about him until now."

"Yes, I suppose you are right, Mary. Sometimes no news is good news. Did I tell you that the engraver chap is coming here tomorrow? He still has the details and format for Wesley's headstone on record and he just wants to confirm that I want the same again."

"I suppose it is important to put down the right wording." Mary said dreamily. "You can hardly rub it out and start again."

"I could always give him my name to add to it, Mary. Just tell him to leave the date blank for now." Valetta said mischievously.

"Oh really, Mrs Johns, what an idea." Mary said in mock criticism.

"I shall get an estimate from this man," Valetta continued.

"Of the price, dear, or the missing date?" Mary said, sending Mrs Johns into hoots of laughter.

"Really, Mary Ainsworth, you are worse than me."

The ladies enjoyed their afternoon together in the sunshine until Mary took the glasses indoors and set about preparing Valetta's evening meal. It was part of the

THE TALE OF THE OLD SCHOOL TIES

daily ritual that Mary would have the meal ready for six o'clock, allowing Valetta to watch the early evening news as she ate. This done, Mary would normally leave for home and today would be no different.

The body of Morton Grant had been released for burial by the Procurator Fiscal and Fleming had joined Hamish MacLeod, Douglas Campbell and Darren Black at the service. The church was full, a small comfort to Celia Kirkwood and a clear indication of how Morton had touched the hearts of everyone without him ever openly attaching himself to anyone. A remarkable man was how the clergyman described him and few would disagree.

Sunny evening or not, Mary Ainsworth had closed and locked the patio doors before leaving. She suspected that Valetta could drop off to sleep after dinner and that would not help her to be safe.

It was after eight o'clock when Valetta stirred in her chair and looked around her for some sense of how things were. She removed her tray from her lap to the floor, looked across at the patio doors and then at the clock on the wall. She had either missed the news at six o'clock, or maybe she had simply forgotten what was said. She had finished her meal after all. She rose and went to fetch her large knitting bag from the shelf in the corner of the room. It appeared to be full of balls of wool and some current knitting project but the truth was that Valetta had not knitted anything for several weeks. She could not knit tonight either but wanted to have the knitting bag on her lap as she watched the popular drama on television. It began at nine o'clock.

It was shortly after eleven when Valetta was quite engrossed in the story that the pulsating circle appeared in the top left corner of her screen. She hurriedly grasped the remote control and pressed the red button. In the multiplex display she could see a figure outside her patio doors. She pressed button 2 and zoomed in on the figure. He had no mask or hat and despite his untidy appearance she had no doubt as to his identity.

"Harvey, oh no, please God, make him go away," she pleaded, her frail hand slipping into the knitting bag. Outside she could see that Bertram Harvey Johns was looking for something. He approached the patio doors and tried the handle. From her chair Valetta could see the handle being depressed and the outline of her son silhouetted against the glass.

As soon as the first blow struck and fractured the glass there was the piercing scream of a siren and lights outside began to flash in a dramatic fashion, but Harvey Johns was not deterred. He repeatedly struck the glass until he had burst enough of the toughened glass for him to squeeze through, his eyes wide in crazed excitement. In his hands he now held a white rope, his father's lanyard, stolen from this house on his previous visit. He held the rope taut between his hands as he stared directly at his mother and moved towards her.

Valetta Johns called out to him, "No, Harvey, no," as the wild-eyed intruder savoured every advancing step. She did not allow him to get too close. She saw in front of her a crazed sadistic killer, not her son Harvey. She lifted the service pistol from the knitting bag and calmly pointed it at Harvey and squeezed the trigger. At this range and with her ability to keep it together under pressure, Valetta Johns could not miss. Her son stopped as he jerked a little and remained upright momentarily before falling forwards onto the floor, his head almost reaching his mother's feet.

Someone was knocking frantically at the front door. Then several people seemed to be knocking. Someone called her name. There seemed to be a debate as to whether a shot had been fired. Valetta stayed in her chair, holding the pistol and looking down at her son. That was when the first police officer vaulted his way into the back garden and looked tentatively through the broken doors.

The month of August was able to maintain the spell of good weather in the west highlands and Andrew Fleming was able to take Mary and the children to a small chalet in Wester Ross for a summer break. There was a clear blue sea to swim in and broad beaches of sand known only to locals where private picnics could be enjoyed at any time and peace was the key to it all.

All too soon the peace was over and Fleming returned

to Corran Bay and a less peaceful dayshift. He was sitting at a desk writing up initial reports on two road accidents that had happened that morning, when MacKellar came into the room.

"This parcel came for you when you were on holiday, Andrew. It is addressed to you at the office but I've no idea what it is."

Fleming thought it entirely unnecessary that the Chief Inspector should know what it was. MacKellar's ignorance of the contents was obviously the only reason he was delivering Fleming's mail by hand. He just stood there, not going away.

Fleming looked at the box, approximately six inches cubed and marked with a London postmark. He took a small penknife from his pocket and sliced through the parcel tape. MacKellar frowned in disapproval of the knife but said nothing.

When he opened the box Fleming found a brand new tie in a cellophane sleeve. The tie was dark green with diagonal gold stripes. The accompanying letter had a background of a faintly depicted country mansion house and was headed, 'Brackston Hall, Utterley Park, Kent'. The hand-written letter read,

'Dear Constable Fleming, I must commend you in the strongest possible terms for bringing to a satisfactory conclusion a long chapter of misery and injustice.

On behalf of the Board of Trustees for the Letherford School for Boys, and for myself on a personal level, please accept this small token of gratitude and recognition for the service you have done us all

Yours sincerely, Charles Greenwell."

"Who is Charles Greenwell?" MacKellar asked with a hint of annoyance.

"My dear friend, Lord Brackston," Fleming replied, as if he had known the man for years.

The author is retired but his professional life was spent in law enforcement. An operational career in Scottish police forces was followed by roles in private health security, aviation security, civil law process and Scots Law proofing.

He is a husband, father and grandfather and now resides in Edinburgh.

GEORGE MURRAY BOOKS

Justice for Jenny and Judas

Evil Issue

Blind Love Blind Hate

<u>The Fleming Series</u>

The Weed Killer

Mrs Livingstone's Legacy

A Tale of Old Comrades